The Grainger Market Murders

Barry Hindson

First published in Great Britain in 2021

All characters and events in this publication, other than those clearly in the public domain, are fictitious and any resemblance to real persons, living or dead, is purely coincidental.

Typeset in Minion Pro

Credit and copyright for cover design Marcus Reed.
Design, typesetting and publishing by UK Book Publishing
www.ukbookpublishing.com

ISBN: 978-1-914195-13-6

Dedicated to the memories of
Charlotte Maguire and Lilian Hindson
Uncle Harry and Uncle Bob

Kaleidoscope

THIS RECOLLECTION of my experience on the night of 31st May 2018 is as accurate as I am able to recall of what was a hallucination. I had never in my life had an experience remotely like it.

The chemo treatment was the first in a series of six. The purpose was to reinforce the quarterly injections I was now receiving for the prostate cancer with which I had been diagnosed a month earlier. The hope was that a combination of the two would help combat the disease and give me an extension of maybe six years without noticeable change in my general well-being. It seemed a good option as I am now in my mid-70s. So, the game was afoot.

The nurses who had administered the hour-long drip of liquid into my arm to which I had been subjected had warned me of a range of potential side effects which I could expect to experience. I thought I was prepared; complacent, even, after four days and no reaction. Maybe I would be one of the fortunate few who escaped the side effects.

The first sign of impending doom came on the fifth day, when a particularly malevolent attack of diarrhoea began and remained my constant companion for four subsequent days. It eventually eased, to my literal and emotional relief, but its understudy stepped dutifully in from the wings, when I was beset by one of the more common side effects of the chemotherapy in the form of nausea and hiccups.

This had clearly been anticipated by the chemo unit, where I had been issued in advance with tablets to combat the condition. I swallowed one of the pills, hoping to settle down for a decent night's sleep. I had been sleeping badly since I had embarked on my first session of chemotherapy.

Alas, the tablets provided relatively scant relief and the lack of sleep was becoming an issue. My nurse suggested a different and more potent variety of tablet and expressed her confidence in its ability to solve the problem. She also issued me with a codicil to the effect that this was a potent remedy. I was on no account to exceed the stated dose. So, that night I took myself to bed in good time, read for a few minutes, then took the tablet. It certainly looked impressive; striking green and midnight black in colour. Haloperidol was the name under which it masqueraded.

I extinguished the bedside lamp, lay my head on the pillow and turned towards the bay window. Then I closed my eyes. What followed was the most extraordinary experience of my life.

Instantly, and without warning, the room and walls assumed an expanding cycloramic effect of midnight blue sky and myriad silver stars. Then the room began to expand elliptically and very quickly. It seemed to become part of the surrounding environment.

My first reaction was one of bewilderment. I felt no fear, maybe a little apprehension, but no feeling at all of threat. There was a naturalness about my mood which made me feel comfortable and safe.

As I sat up in bed, two people dressed in high collared cloaks joined me and sat on my left, the nearest placing a hand very gently on my shoulder. I had no notion of who they were, but I experienced an inexorable feeling of warmth and safety in their presence. I felt they were integral to the experience of which I was beginning to be a part; maybe even responsible for its creation in some way.

There followed a spellbinding explosion of vibrant colour and movement; then music, upbeat and cheerfully lively, but not too loud. The sky became alive. There were unconventional figures larger than life, dressed in lurid costumes. They were unusual in appearance; not threatening, but nevertheless a fundamental part of this developing kaleidoscope.

Then came strange craft, large and small, fast and slow, bright and vibrant, dragging my eyes this way and that. Fantasy animals of multi-hues and circus characters, all culminating in a cornucopia of visual wonder. It was a spellbinding fantasia, a flamboyant extravaganza, a Shangri-La.

There was nothing of quackery, falsehood, caprice or hocus-pocus here; nothing of the mountebank, no posture. This was purity, elegant and graceful. It was profound, yet whimsical, a combination of burlesque, pantomime, harlequinade, masque and pageant. It was unique and awe-inspiring and the absurdity was, it all seemed to be for my benefit.

Gradually the scene began to alter and fade. My two companions and myself stood up and stepped out into the evening and my thoughts turned to the Darling children in Peter Pan. We floated with no sense of urgency, but in a particular and familiar direction towards the centre of Newcastle.

We came to rest in the otherwise empty showroom of a large shop located at the junction of Market Street and Grainger Street. We took our seats on a large white sofa. The bay window of the showroom followed the camber of the road, curving in a gentle arc. As the roads merged, we were provided with perfect views of Grey's Monument to the right and the magnificent, slow-motion elegance of what appeared to be 1930s Grainger Street to our left. It was all too sophisticated, vivid and complex to be a dream. My past experience was that my dreams had been inconsistent, disjointed and erratic, without continuity and regularity. They were fleeting and seldom fluent. What I was experiencing now was a hallucination.

In the street, well-to-do ladies in fur collared full-length coats accompanied by gentlemen in Crombie overcoats with velvet collars, walked arm in arm, lingering at shop windows, occasionally stepping inside to make a purchase. Across the road, street traders were plying their wares from stalls in front of the Grainger Market; hot drinks of mulled wine, cocoa, hot chocolate and coffee. Snacks and pork rolls, saveloys and roast chestnuts all lending their distinctive aromas to the evening air. It seemed to be that it was approaching Christmas and the spirits and smells of the season were manifesting themselves.

The high-class stores behind the refreshment stalls had their street-level lights shining on dresses and scarves, coats and accessories. On the first floor, restaurants were serving early supper to couples and families. On the level above the restaurants, balcony windows opened and women in glittering gowns were dancing with gentlemen in evening suits to the music of Johann Strauss and Franz Lehar, while on the illuminated roofs a rumble-tumble of entertainment burst into boisterous life.

Circus performers; jugglers, tumblers, clowns and unicyclists, combined and competed with variety and theatre novelty and specialist acts. They were supplemented by singing buskers. Firecrackers were punctuating the air, exploding into noisy flashes of bright colour which lit the darkening sky with glorious abandon.

It was the most splendid and spectacular entertainment extravaganza. The continuity of it all, for that is what it seemed to be, with its lavish presentation and production values, its cast of hundreds, the music, costumes, entertainment and above all the colour, was enchanting. It was like a high-quality film production.

The whole scene was phenomenal, flabbergasting, awe-inspiring and it felt as though the amazing cornucopia had a purpose. The curious and enchanting thing was that I had the impression I was an honoured guest. This whole experience seemed to me, to be for my benefit.

To this point I had not spoken, not even to my two close companions who were keeping a watching brief. Then I was finally moved to say; 'There are no buses.' On cue, two small showfolk buses, incongruously constructed in neon, parp-parped gently around Market Street and past our viewpoint. How was that for extempore thinking and action?

The two little neon buses were absurd in the context; a

spontaneous response which bore no relationship to the surrounding environment. However, they reflected the kind of sparkling fun and mischief which only two people had shown me in my life with any consistency: Mam and Nana. Those buses may well have been an indication of where this whole experience was coming from.

If they were responsible, it explained almost everything and gave it completeness. It brought me love and joy at a crucial time. Maybe they were unable to reveal their identity, but they trusted me to know who they were. Perhaps the enormity and grandeur of what they had achieved and created was the ultimate indication of their regard for me and my well-being at this difficult time. I had no way of knowing beyond my instinct and maybe that was why it seemed inappropriate to strike up a conversation.

By now it was becoming dusk and the pedestrians were beginning to wend their way to their carriages and homeward transport. The glorious colours of earlier dimmed, the shop and streetlights now wintery and misty oranges and yellows. Across the way. the stallholders and hawkers were packing up and adjourning to the Grainger Market to prepare for the morrow. The roof show was over, the diners had left, replete like the dancers. The street cleaners began to appear and there was a growing sense of closure. The show in all its splendour was over, so what now?

Again, I wondered what my role in all this, and that of my companions, had been. In answer to my unarticulated question, my main companion for the evening leaned across and asked;

'Was it all right?'

'It was miraculous. Glorious, happy, cheering up fun. Thank you so much,' I replied, heartfelt.

We drifted back across the skyline, leaving the seasonal splendour of Grainger Street and its environs behind, as well as the amazing and unforgettable experience I had just witnessed.

My two companions each gave me a brief, loving hug which exuded that special warmth loved ones share. Then, sadly they were gone. It was over, but it would never be over.

In a short time, I was back in my bed. I tried to put some meaning to my experience. This whole pageant of delights had to be much more than a sequence of randomness. It had to have a meaning which was special to me. As I reflected, and as I should have expected, meaning came.

CHAPTER ONE

TUESDAY, 2ND OCTOBER, 1934

IT WAS twenty past seven in the morning. The overnight darkness persisted, it's chill seeping into the October morning as Bob Frame leaned against the pitch black, carbon ingrained archway which opened on the bottom of Bulmer Street – a typical town-centre tenement terrace – on to Gallowgate.

Bob was listening for the echoing of sturdy footwear on the damp and slippery cobblestones and the gentle whistling of a popular song of the day; sure signs that his friend, neighbour and work colleague, Detective Sergeant Harry Maguire, was on his way down the street. Together they would complete the short walk into town to the magnificent new police station on Market Street which had opened earlier that year.

Detective Constable Bob Frame was a Scotsman from the tough Maryhill area of Glasgow. Despite its relatively small size and population, Maryhill had developed a notorious reputation for lawlessness arising from an excess of alcohol consumption in the Victorian era. So much so that it became the first area in Britain to support a branch of the Temperance movement.

However, since those days the community had become

a successful industrial area where employment levels were high and it was now an area of closely-knit families of which the Frames was one. Bob grew up as one of three children. He showed an early aptitude for carrying out repairs on cars and the indications were that he would remain in Maryhill and work in the motor trade. It came as a major shock when he informed his family he had been accepted to join the police force. This he did by using the dubious but effective trick of buying a pair of built-up shoes to achieve the minimum height which was required by police regulations. In 1930 he applied successfully to join the detective division and he seemed set for a steady career on the force, where his conscientious approach to his work had not gone unnoticed by his superiors. He was also perceptive and was known to see the crux of a matter when others struggled.

It was by chance while he was holidaying in Whitley Bay he met his future wife, Ena. It quickly became apparent they were meant for each other and the upshot was that Bob applied for a transfer to Newcastle. Six months later he and Ena married and they moved into the flat below Ena's parents in Bulmer Street. They soon had a son, Dennis, and Bob was firmly and permanently settled on Tyneside, happy in his job as a Detective Constable.

Bob puffed on his first cigarette of the day with professional proficiency a couple of times and, as he stamped his feet on the cobbles in mitigation against the weather, he heard the door to number 20 closing, followed by Harry's distinctive, loping footsteps as the sound of the current Fats Waller hit, 'Honeysuckle Rose', wafted across the dark and dreary morning.

CHAPTER ONE

Like Bob and Ena, Harry and Doris Maguire lived in the same street as their previous generation. Ted and Charlotte Maguire occupied number 27. Despite the unusual housing arrangements of the two families, they did not live in each other's pockets. It was true they would invariably meet up in the Ordnance Arms at the bottom of Bulmer Street for a couple of beers and two hours of socialising on Saturday night, but Harry and Bob were work colleagues first and friends second.

Unlike Bob, Harry was a local Newcastle lad, the youngest of four children with three older sisters, Nancy, Lily and Tilly. He had been married to Doris for a couple of years and they had a small son, Stephen, and another child on the way. He, too, was settled in both his domestic situation and his work life, Harry Maguire was a tall man, almost six feet in height and he looked the part of an up and coming detective with his upright bearing and commanding appearance. Thoughtful and perceptive, he was adept at taking a breath before making a decision. Even-tempered, he had rarely been seen to show anger. A keen footballer, he turned out for the force team when his work and family commitments allowed.

Harry had made rapid progress since he had joined the police. His success rate was impressive and he was highly regarded and recognised as a natural leader; he and Bob made a good team.

The two men set off for work, striding down Gallowgate, across Percy Street and down Blackett Street. As they walked down Nelson Street, Harry allowed himself an inward smile when they passed the Gaiety Cinema, known in local parlance as the 'Pie and Tatie.' He had spent many happy boyhood evenings there enjoying a free show from the cheapest seats in exchange for a jam jar or a lemonade bottle which the cinema manager was able to recycle. The distinguished author, Charles Dickens had appeared on six occasions at the Gaiety in its music hall days, reading from his works. He remarked that the Newcastle audience was 'the best in England,' though whether that was a gratuitous line he used to curry favour wherever he performed or a genuine compliment is a matter of speculation.

After a brisk ten-minute stroll, Harry and Bob left the discouraging, miserable weather behind them as they passed through the entrance of the splendidly impressive new police station, pride of the city in its imposing and sturdy splendour. They called a cheery greeting to the ubiquitous desk sergeant, before making their way downstairs to the canteen for a quick cup of tea to dispel the chill. Twenty minutes later they were heading up the imposing marble staircase to the first floor where the small detective unit was based.

As they approached the door of the Chief Superintendent's office, it was opened from the inside. An extremely tall and painfully thin man, pale of complexion and sporting a carefully trimmed pencil moustache and looking immaculate in the uniform of his rank, stepped into the corridor, bustling with business. Without preamble, the man whose appearance had earned him the nickname of 'the Spectre,' beckoned the two men in his direction;

'In here, you two.'

Bob and Harry exchanged quick glances. Most mornings they managed to get past the door of the boss's office before it opened. Even on the occasions when they fell at this particular Becher's Brook, the greeting was usually fairly relaxed by the standards of police protocol. The implication of this morning's brusque instruction was not lost on them. Something was up.

Detective Chief Superintendent Wallace Kennedy 'Ken' Walton came straight to the point

'There has been a murder in the Grainger Market. Unfortunately, our current detective force consists of you two bright sparks and me. We have no Detective Superintendent, the Chief Inspector is on long term sick leave and we are waiting to appoint a Detective Inspector. It is a long way from being an ideal situation, but it is the one in which we find ourselves. I am therefore assigning the case to you two. You are good lads and good detectives and I am trusting you to solve it for us. If we can pull it off it will be a great coup for the station, and I think you are up to it. I am not looking for any help from beyond the City Force at present.

'A temporary Incident Room has been set up in Alley No. 3 in the market in Unit 130. The victim is a 23-year- old florist by the name of Mary Bartlett. It looks like she has been stabbed and found in a chair in Conlon's flower shop which is Unit 101. The fingerprint man is there and George Howes, the police surgeon, is on his way. So, get yourselves over there and don't let me down. I will set up the Incident Room here.'

He held out the case notes to Harry.

'Here is the file, such as it is. Get cracking.'

CHAPTER TWO

TUESDAY, 2ND OCTOBER

THE TWO officers left Chief Superintendent Walton's office in something of a daze. The boss's instructions had come entirely out of the blue and they took some coming to terms with.

'Good grief, Bob, what do you make of this lot?' Harry exclaimed.

'It's certainly a challenge, but Walton's right. If we can pull this off, we will be the toast of the station. We won't know how demanding the case is likely to be until we get over to the Grainger Market and assess the lie of the land, of course, but, with a bit of luck, it could be routine. Maybe the result of a lover's tiff, for instance, or possibly an attempted burglary of the shop gone wrong. On the other hand, it could be tricky; no prints, no clues, no obvious suspects. We'll just have to hope for the best, Guv.'

(From the first day they had worked together on the force, Bob Frame, scrupulous as he was and always guided by a desire to do things the proper way, had drawn a clear margin between his working relationship with Harry Maguire and the fact that they were also neighbours and friends who socialised together in their off-duty moments.

To avoid awkwardness, therefore, he had taken it upon himself to address Harry by his first name when they were not working but to use the common police term 'Guv' when they were on duty. This acknowledged Harry's superior rank and avoided any awkwardness. It was not an issue which they had discussed, as Bob had pre-empted any potential problem by making his own rule and Harry accepted the situation without comment.)

Both Harry and Bob had some previous experience of working on murder investigations but neither had been designated a leading role. They were both aware of the protocols and procedures from their training. However, this would be their first opportunity to exchange the words in the handbook for the practical responsibilities of chief investigators. While both men had confidence in their own abilities and full trust in their partners, this was virgin territory. As Bob rightly said, they would find out soon enough the nature of the task which lay before them.

'Come on then, Bob, let's get over there and take a look.'

The two murder squad rookies set off from the station on the five-minute walk down Market Street to the junction with Grainger Street, the nearest entrance to the Grainger Market and the scene of the crime. Opened in 1838, having been designed by Richard Grainger as a major feature of the developing Grainger Town area, which was intended as a showpiece section of the town centre, the Grainger Market was conceived primarily for trading in meat. It was opened with great pomp and ceremony with a lavish celebratory dinner. 2,000 men including Grainger and the other major influence on the architecture of the city, John Dobson, were in attendance, paying up to five shillings a head for food and wine. Incredibly, four hundred ladies were permitted to attend purely as spectators. They were restricted to a viewing gallery which they were required to share with the orchestra. You can imagine the reaction of the women of today such as Doris and Ena if they were asked to subject themselves to that kind of indignity!

Unfortunately, the designers had over-estimated the demand for the numbers of butchers who would require permits and in order to guarantee the success of the venture, it was found necessary to extend the range of vendors who were able to apply for permission to trade. At first, fruit and vegetable purveyors began to spring up in a specially designated area, and eventually, individual tradespeople began to rent stalls. Shoe repairers, florists, plant sellers, jewellers, cheese purveyors and bakers all rented space. The need to diversify proved to be the making of the market. The range of goods and services on sale and the low prices as a consequence of fierce competition, combined to attract a wider clientele and to create the thriving shopping arcade the Grainger Market is today.

The market was starting to come to life as Harry and Bob made their way towards their temporary Incident Room. The stall-holders were beginning arranging their fruit and vegetable displays with due diligence, showing off their produce to best effect. Banter between would-be sellers and potential customers was being ramped up. Shopping in the market was a social affair, with women on limited budgets searching for the best buys, conscious of quality as well as price.

Neighbours recognised each other and paused for a chat and the atmosphere was convivial, much enhanced by the chirpy patter and cheerful exchange of greetings which added genuine vibrancy and good humour to the proceedings; 'Morning Florrie love, how are the bairns?… what can I get you today love?…how about some nice cox's pippins and a couple of slices of melon for the little 'uns?… sweet as honey and cheap as chips…lovely ripe tomatoes there, lasses…perfect for hoying at the old man if he worksheself…stewing steak, hinny, best on the market… real Scotch beef, walked all the way doon from Aberdeen just for you, pet…look at these taties… You won't find better…perfect for roasting or chips…divvent listen to him, missus, buy mine, they're much bigger and tastier, honest… carrots, ripe carrots…help you see in the dark they will… you'll be able to spot a fly in the netty door…' It was all good-hearted fun and it was a daily feature of life in the market. Even the fishmongers joined in with a quip or two;

'Fresh haddock, ladies…swimmin' in the North Sea last neet, they were…what aboot some lovely whiting…melts in the mooth…fancy a couple of cod fillets, pet…you know how he loves fish and chips…give him a treat and he'll be chasing you round the kitchen table…' The banter was part and parcel of the market shopping experience and it made for a great, friendly atmosphere.

'Here we are,' Harry said, 'Alley 3, Unit 130. This is our base. That looks like the scene of crime across the way.' Two young police constables stood trying to look authoritative as Bob and Harry arrived at the florists.

'Morning, 'Constable Lloyd, Constable Doyle. Anything

happening?'

PC Lloyd, a fresh-faced, slimly built young man with an earnest expression and a willingness to please was the first to react;

'Yes, sir. The fingerprint man has had a look around and is waiting to speak to you and the police surgeon, Mr. Howes, has just finished examining the body. They are both waiting in the Incident Room.'

'Good lad.'

Before taking up their places in the Incident Room, Harry and Bob stepped into the florists to carry out a brief examination of the scene of the crime. It was a chilling experience. Surrounded by wreaths and other floral tributes waiting to be collected for someone's funeral later, presumably, there was a plain white chair with a wicker back and seat. The corpse of Mary Bartlett was sitting up in the chair, almost as though she had been placed there as part of a ritual. Apart from bloodstains on her chest, and further bloodstains on the floor behind her, which indicated the manner in which she had met her fate, she looked normal and natural and the scene had a painful impact on both officers.

'Not the kind of thing you want to see, Bob,' was Harry's reaction, 'It looks like a tableau and you almost expect the poor girl to say hello.'

'I agree,' his colleague responded, 'whoever arranged this was a cool customer. Anyone could have been passing and caught the killer in the act.'

'Let's hope so; our job will be a lot easier if we can find a witness.'

They were about to make their way across the alley when PC Lloyd cleared his throat tentatively to speak again;

'Excuse me, Sarge, there is also a lady to see you in the Incident Room. Her name is Mrs. Conlon and she owns the florist's shop where the body was discovered. In fact, it was her who found it and she is in a bit of a state.'

'Right. We'll see her straight away. One of you stay put. The other go around the units nearest the scene of crime. See if you can find anyone who was working late last night and if they were, ask them to come to the Incident Room and give us the details. Okay? You never know, someone might have seen something useful.'

Harry and Bob crossed the alley purposefully to Unit 130, opened the door and stepped inside. The first person they spoke to was Maurice Lackenby, the fingerprint expert.

The collection of prints is based on the use of a fine black powder the particles of which adhere by suction to fingers and palms. It is a particularly skilled and subtle process, and a top fingerprint expert is a major asset to the modern police force. Unfortunately, professional criminals have already learned to avoid detection by protecting their hands with gloves. However, the fact is most murders are unpremeditated, and the perpetrators are frequently apprehended because they do not cover their hands to protect themselves from the fingerprint man's skills.

Maurice Lackenby was as flamboyant and bohemian in appearance as he was scrupulous and meticulous in his work. A tall and rotund individual, his face was dominated by a flowing handlebar moustache and a pair of bushy and untrimmed eyebrows. His nose was prominent and his eyes, while they held the hint of a twinkle, were penetrating and focussed. His hair was unfashionably long and unkempt and the whole impression he gave was of an extrovert character.

He greeted Harry Maguire with his customary bonhomie, though the outcome of his careful examination of the crime scene proved not to be encouraging;

'Good day, young Harry,' he boomed in the stentorian tones which perfectly complemented his physical appearance, 'a bad business, this, dear boy. The place is covered with prints, as you would expect from a busy shop with a regular clientele. Unfortunately, from our perspective, however, there are no prints on the body or the chair in which it was found.'

'What are you saying, Maurice? Is there nothing positive you can give to help build our case?'

'Afraid not, dear boy. I also dusted the door handle, for which I had hopes, but any prints there might have been were obliterated when the owner opened the door and discovered the body. She was wearing gloves. Sorry Harry, but I can't offer you any glimmer of encouragement I fear.

'Maurice Lackenby was acknowledged to be one of the best in the business, and if he could find no significant prints, the fact was that no such prints existed. Harry had no option but to thank him for his efforts and turn his attention to the police surgeon.

George Howes stood at the far wall, waiting his turn. He routinely attended violent or unexpected deaths in the city and carried out post-mortems. A Sunderland man, he was 'old school.' Quietly spoken and polite in the extreme, he was highly regarded in the Newcastle station and generally recognised as being very capable. He was a crucial member of the team and could be entirely depended upon to discover anything relevant.

'Ah, Harry, how pleasant,' he greeted Maguire. 'How are you?'

'I hope you can be more helpful than Lackenby, George,' said Harry 'What have you got for us?'

Conscious of the lady in the room who had earlier introduced herself to him as the shop owner, George was cautious in his response;

'I am taking the body away and I should be able to give you some useful information tomorrow morning at the post-mortem. I have to rush but I would expect to be ready for you at about 10:30, all being well.'

'That soon? Exceptional service as usual, George.' Harry couldn't resist a smile in Bob's direction. George Howes was a busy man and a top-class practitioner in his field. The fact that he seemed confident of delivering his results in his usual prompt and immaculate fashion was encouraging. It certainly boosted the spirits of the two detectives. There were no fingerprints, but this was promising news from George. Now for Pauline Conlon.

CHAPTER THREE

TUESDAY, 2ND OCTOBER

On the face of it, Pauline Conlon had everything going for her. She had been married to Davy Conlon, a successful and wealthy street bookmaker in the city centre, since they were in their early twenties. Both from the West End of Newcastle, they were strong characters and possessed good trading acumen and this was reflected in the success of their individual businesses. They had reached the point where Davy's bookmaking activities and Pauline's florist's shop had been thriving for several years.

Now in his fifties, Davy had been involved in street betting all his working life. He began as a bookie's runner when he left school, before establishing himself in his own right. He was a tough businessman who had prospered rapidly. He was extremely hard working and possessed a ruthless streak which he was not afraid to exploit if the situation demanded it. As a result, he was the living proof of the commonly held myth that you never saw a poor bookmaker.

As a wedding present, he had bought Pauline an extended lease on a unit in the Grainger Market, which she intended to open as a florist's shop. He bankrolled her for a couple of years until such time as she found her feet. Pauline, though, was cut from the same cloth as her husband and she learned her trade quickly and well. She soon established a very successful business of her own.

Pauline was a bright woman and she identified the flaws in her husband's character from early in their marriage. She also recognised and understood his need to cut corners in his business. There were hazards and pitfalls to be avoided in the betting game and he needed to be devious as well as conscientious to succeed. That was something of which she was aware and even encouraged. After all, business was business and if he was successful and accumulated a healthy bank balance, she was likely to be the prime beneficiary.

His cavalier view of the sanctity of marriage was an entirely different matter. He was not handsome by any means, but this did not prevent him from portraying himself as a ladies' man. Pauline obviously did not approve. However, she realised eventually he was not going to be a faithful husband, no matter what she said or did to discourage him. Instead, she fell back on the pragmatic view that if he was exploiting his penchant for a pretty or willing companion somewhere else, at least he was not bothering her.

It was not a surprise that the marriage had produced no children. Neither partner possessed any real parental instincts and while it was never a topic of extended or serious discussion between then, there was an unspoken understanding that their focus was to be on achieving success and building wealth in their respective businesses.

Not a natural beauty herself, Pauline made the best

of her resources. Inclined to a fuller figure, she had her clothes made by an accomplished seamstress in town who knew how to disguise any excesses in her silhouette. She dressed expensively and well and if her taste was inclined to the extravagant, she managed to stay just about on the right side of 'common.' Pauline was a strong-willed woman who was never afraid to speak her mind. She sprinkled her conversations liberally with swearing and profanity, particularly when she was angry or upset. She ruffled feathers from time to time, but her reputation for bluntness and plain speaking meant that people were not inclined to take liberties with her. People knew where they stood with Pauline Conlon.

With the passage of time, Pauline's marriage to Davy became a thing of convenience and she focused her talents and energies on her increasingly successful business. She worked diligently and drove her staff hard, though she rewarded them well. She also had a reputation for providing value for money which was well justified. In addition, she had a natural aptitude for flower arrangement which ensured a more or less constant demand to provide floral tributes for funerals and wedding bouquets.

While she drove a hard bargain in her dealings with wholesalers and suppliers, any financial benefits she accrued as a result were used to supplement a product which could be met by the pockets of people on modest as well as extravagant budgets. It was a shrewd strategy and it stood her in good stead. All-in-all, Conlon's Florists had the bases very well covered.

Like her husband, Pauline enjoyed the good things of life

and while they were both flamboyant people and Davy's excesses were seldom hidden, she led a life which remained on the right side of respectability. Unlike her husband, she was not prone to indulgences with the opposite sex. Despite the provocations she endured because of his dalliances, she remained faithful. She preferred to pamper herself with weekly visits to the hairdresser, the beautician and the manicurist. There may have been a level of artificiality to her appearance, but she worked very hard to cultivate the public persona of a successful businesswoman who owned a flourishing florist's shop in the centre of town, which was exactly what she was.

Pauline cut a forlorn and distraught figure when the two police constables who had been delegated to the scene of crime escorted her across the Alley and gave her a seat in the Incident Room to await their superiors. She had been sitting waiting in miserable solitude for some time, there being no females on the Newcastle force who could have been assigned to keep her company.

Harry and Bob arrived and introduced themselves. It was not the first time Harry had lamented the absence of women police officers. He considered the practice to be out-moded and the appropriate reform to be long overdue. He was acutely aware that neither Bob or himself possessed the necessary skills to offer Mrs. Conlon the compassion and comfort the situation required. A woman's touch would have been most useful. Although she was still in a shocked and distressed state, she dried her eyes and made a visible effort to compose herself as she saw Harry and Bob approaching. Not for the first time, the judicious application of make-up helped, and despite the trauma of having come across the murdered corpse of her employee, she declared herself fit to give her account of events in response to Detective Constable Frame's questions.

'I can only imagine how stressful this must be for you Mrs. Conlon, and I know you will understand we need to ask you some questions to help us understand what happened here. Can you begin by telling us about the circumstances in which you found the body?'

'I can't really imagine what happened to be honest, Mr. Frame. It's been a massive shock, but I'll do my best for Mary's sake. I came in early at 7:30, as we have a big funeral this morning for Tommy Patterson's wife and I needed to check all the floral tributes. Poor Mary stayed late last night to finish off. She had done it on previous occasions, and I trusted her. I was happy to leave her in charge. She had the spare keys and knew how to lock up when she was finished. She said something about going dancing at the Oxford Galleries later. She used to go there regularly with some of the other girls from the market. It's very respectable there, you know, and the management go to great lengths to see it stays that way.

'Anyway, I went to open the shop door and it was unlocked. I was annoyed I must admit. I stepped into the shop. There is a step down to the actual serving level and I saw Mary sitting in the chair. I thought at first that she was asleep. She was so conscientious, poor lamb, and I thought she must still be tired from last night. It wasn't until I noticed the red patch on the front of her dress that I realised something was seriously wrong.'

Mrs. Conlon was rattling through her account, anxious to tell it as quickly as possible without losing her composure, but she was starting to struggle as the impact of the morning's events began to hit home again;

'I spoke to her, of course, but when she didn't reply I ran straight next door to Eddie White's, the butcher's. I was in a right bloody state, I don't mind telling you. I asked him to come and have a look at her, him being used to dead things with his work. He knew straight away...'

Mrs. Conlon stopped talking. Despite her valiant efforts, her composure was taken over by distress. Bob gave her a clean handkerchief and she dabbed it carefully under her eyes, careful not to disturb her mascara. She took some sips of water from a glass he handed to her. The officers waited patiently until she nodded to indicate she was ready to resume.

'It must have been a huge shock,' Bob prompted.

'It was. You have no idea, It is not what you expect, is it? Not in your own bloody shop with one of your own staff. The market is a friendly place, and everybody knows each other. A lot of the shop and stall staff come to work here straight from leaving school and there is a lovely atmosphere. Most of the customers are regulars and the patter is great. Quite a lot of the stalls are family run and some have been in the same hands for generations. People respect each other. There's always a buzz about the place. I am afraid this business will devastate everyone.'

'So, then you got in touch with us?'

'I told Eddie to. I was in no fit state. I was nee good to be honest. I hope I did the right thing.

'Of course you did, Mrs. Conlon. You have been very brave and very helpful. Thank you.'

At this point Detective Sergeant Harry Maguire took over the interview;

'I need to ask you some more general questions Mrs. Conlon, if you can manage it. I would like you to tell me everything you know about Mary Bartlett. The clearer the picture we have, the better it will be for us to work out what happened. Let me begin by asking how long Mary had been with you.'

'She came to me straight from leaving school. I know Miss Cooper, the Headmistress, and I asked her if she could recommend a respectable, bright and hard-working lass I could train up as a florist. She suggested Mary without hesitation. She told me she lived with her mother who was a widow and they were decent people. Mrs. Bartlett worked as a cleaner at the school and, by all accounts, she was honest and trustworthy as well as hard working. They lived on Stanton Street, so Mary was only ten minutes' walk from home to here. It would be no problem for her to travel to work and back

'Miss Cooper also said Mary was artistic and she had one of her pictures hanging on the wall in the school hall. She would be able to cope easily with the creative side of the work. She seemed ideal, so I had her in for a natter. She was a canny lass, pleasant and confident without being pushy. She was also polite and answered the questions I put to her in a common-sense way. I was particularly impressed by the way in which she talked about hoping she would be good enough to work on the floral side, as well as being a shop assistant. I like young people who show ambition. but she was not over-confident or owt like that. I took to her straight away. She started work just a week after leaving school.'

'And how did she take to it?'

'Well, she was a bit nervous at first. I am a bit of a tartar where work is concerned, Mr. Maguire, and I set high standards. I divvent suffer fools, but once Mary realised she could do the work and that I would overlook her mistakes if she didn't repeat them, she was fine. She was a quick learner. She had flair, she listened to the tips and advice I gave her, and she improved each year she was here.'

'Did she have any particular strengths, would you say?'

'As far as the flowers went, she was outstanding with wreaths. Her sense of colour and texture was a natural thing and I could leave her to get on with that sort of work on her own almost from the start. It was a big feather in her cap that I had the confidence in her. That was why she was working late last night. There were a couple of wreaths to finish for the Patterson funeral and Mary insisted on completing them herself.'

'So, you had no problem letting her stay late and locking up when she had finished?'

'Not at all. As I say, she had done it before and she knew the routine.'

'You said she was going dancing later.'

'Aye, she was meeting Betty Forster, who was her best friend and who works for Mickler and Goldberg, the jewellers on the other side of the Market. Betty's boyfriend, Gordon Hugill, works there as well. They were going with some other friends to the Oxford dance hall in town straight from work.'

'And she was a decent type of girl, you say?

'Oh, aye. She wasn't strait-laced, like, but she was right and proper. She went to church and all that. She wasn't flighty or anything and she wasn't common either. I can't stand common people.'

Harry was amused by the irony of this last observation, and stifled a smile.

'Just one more thing. How was she with the customers? What I am driving at is do you know of anyone she had argued with or had made a complaint about her?'

'Not likely! As I say, everybody liked Mary and she was very good at her job. She was always helpful and if it was people coming in to arrange for funeral flowers, she was always kind and sympathetic. She wasn't a gusher, Mr. Maguire. She just treated people properly and if they wanted any advice, she gave it without imposing herself. Really, Sergeant, she was a lovely lass, and she was good at her job. She was an innocent and decent kid and I can't imagine what kind of swine could have done this.'

Pauline's voice cracked and she sniffed back more tears. She was on the edge of breaking down again and Harry was keen to draw things to a conclusion but he had one more question;

'I almost forgot to ask you, did Mary have a boyfriend, Mrs. Conlon?

'Pauline's face clouded over;

'Danny Veitch? Oh yes. I know him and I don't mind telling you, Mary could have done better for herself. He is a butcher here in the market and they reckon he is pretty nifty with a knife. I don't like that sort of thing and he is a cocky sod besides, begging your pardon.'

Harry leaned forward, sensing a potential lead;

'How long have they been seeing each other?'

'Only two or three weeks. To tell you the truth I was hoping it wouldn't last. I didn't trust him, Mr. Maguire. I thought he was a shifty little shit. To be fair, he seemed to treat Mary well enough but there was something about him. I can't put my finger on what it was, but I felt uneasy about him.'

Harry did not respond to this less than flattering analysis of Danny Veitch, beyond noting Pauline's tendency to let her veneer slip into coarseness when she was provoked, and her assessment of Veitch certainly gave him food for thought.

'Okay, we will leave it there for now. Mrs. Conlon. You have been very helpful. If you think of anything else, please let us know. We will keep you informed of any developments and we will need you to come down to the station at some point to sign a written statement, but that can wait until you are over the shock. Thank you very much. Would you like us to arrange some transport to take you home?'

'No, thank you, Mr. Maguire. I have things to see to and I would rather be busy to take my mind off things. If it's all right with you I will pop across to the shop and put the Patterson flowers outside for the funeral people to collect, and when they have been I'll get a taxi home and try to pull myself together. Please catch the bastard who did this terrible thing. Mary didn't deserve it.'

With that, young PC Lloyd was called to escort Mrs. Conlon across the Alley and back to her shop. Thankfully,

Mary Bartlett's corpse had been removed and taken to be prepared for her post-mortem the following day. In due course, she locked the shop and made her way to the taxi rank beside Grey's Monument where, as she had indicated to Harry was her intention, she took a cab to her home in the West End of town.

The interview with Mrs. Conlon had been a testing experience for Harry and Bob and they decided to put the work of the morning on one side. They went upstairs to one of the Market cafes for a bite of lunch and a short spell of relaxation so they could return with fresh minds. It was part of the way they preferred to work that they tried whenever possible to take a short break when they were investigating to clear their heads.

So it was that their lunchtime conversation was centred on the forthcoming Saturday night's boxing bill at New St James's Hall, which featured a healthy sprinkling of local talent. Neither of them was a boxing fanatic, but they both enjoyed the occasional trip to the Hall which, as luck would have it, was just outside the top of Bulmer Street where they lived.

After a substantial plate of mince pie and chips each, a cup of strong tea and a cigarette, they were back in the Incident Room forty five minutes later. Suitably refreshed in mind and body, they were alert and prepared when young PC Lloyd knocked on the door;

'Just to confirm that Mrs. Conlon has gone home sarge. Also, I have some news about the people who were working late last night. There is a man called Hoult, who has a shoemaking and repairing unit. He is coming along in ten minutes, then a Mr. Simpson who has a small-time jewellery business, will be here about half an hour later.'

Harry had almost forgotten his instruction to PC Lloyd to look for people who might have been working late the previous night. The emergence of two people who might have something to add lifted his spirits;

'Good work, Constable. Let me know when they get here.'

'Yes, sarge.'

So, at 2:30 prompt, PC Lloyd knocked on the Incident Room door and announced;

'Mr. Hoult, sarge'.

A tall, angular man with undistinguished features, wearing a brown working overall and with a pencil behind his ear and spectacles balanced on the end of his nose, entered the room, accompanied by a youngster of about fifteen. Raymond Hoult walked slowly and carefully and with obvious discomfort, and he sat down with apparent relief before Harry began the interview.

'Hello, Mr Hoult. I'm DS Maguire and this is DC Frame. We appreciate you coming in. We are trying to build a picture of events last night and I understand you were working late. Anything you might have noticed, however trivial it seems, could be very useful.'

'I understand, officer. I have unit 104 across the way where I make and mend boots and shoes and I was repairing a pair of men's walking shoes. At the same time I was giving some practical training to my apprentice here. This is young Tommy and he's a good lad. I have been trading in the market for 35 years and I like to think I give satisfaction. I locked up just after five to six, and the boy went on ahead of me. He was anxious to get home foe his tea. I have difficulty with arthritis in my hip and I am not so mobile. I made my way across to Market Street as usual to catch the bus. I live in Stannington Grove in Heaton and I always catch the ten past bus.'

'Did you notice anything out of the ordinary, Mr. Hoult?'

'I'm afraid not. It was gloomy and the market was practically deserted.'

'No voices or sounds of scuffling?'

'Nothing at all. I'm sorry I can't be more helpful but as I explained to the constable, I felt it was my duty to come and see you anyway.'

'Not at all, Mr. Hoult. Thanks for taking the trouble. If you wouldn't mind giving us a written statement, you are free to go. If, by any chance you do think of anything else please don't hesitate to let us know. PC Lloyd will take your statement.' Harry turned briefly to the young apprentice;

'Are you able to confirm what Mr. Hoult has told us, Tommy?'

'Yes sir,' was as much as the lad had to offer.

Harry and Bob were satisfied with the shoemaker's account of his movements. If nothing else, his mobility issues and the fact that his apprentice and he provided each other with alibi's ruled them out as suspects. They did not anticipate talking to either Hoult or the lad again.

Almost immediately after the shoemaker's departure there was another knock on the Incident Room door and an altogether more prepossessing and confident figure presented himself. He wore a spotless white shirt, open at the neck, black trousers with seams pressed to razor sharpness and polished shoes that could have graced the dance floor. His thinning black hair gleamed in the artificial light. His over-all appearance was in contrast with the other workers in the market. He stood upright almost in the manner of a soldier on parade and gave the impression of someone who was in control of himself and his actions.

'Good afternoon, gentlemen,' he announced,' my name is Israel Simpson. I have the jewellery shop at Unit 105 and I am responding to your request for anyone who was working late last night to make themselves known to you.'

The two detectives were taken aback somewhat by the articulate and apparently well-educated man who, by comparison with the majority of market workers was immaculate in appearance. As a jeweller he obviously regarded the way he presented himself to the public as important. Bob and Harry were fascinated by Mr. Israel Simpson's natty appearance and found themselves instinctively inclined to pay him a little more attention than they might otherwise have done. They introduced themselves and Harry began by asking Mr. Simpson to explain his movements the previous evening.

'As I said, I have a small jewellery business, just across the Alley only four units along from the flower shop. I sell and repair items of jewellery and I occasionally carry out some specialist work for Mickler and Goldberg, the prestigious jewellery shop on the other side of the market. I was completing a commission for them last evening which is why I was a little late in finishing.'

Harry and Bob pricked up their ears at the mention of Mickler and Goldberg as they were employers of Mary

Bartlett's best friend, Betty Forster.

The Market Supervisor was ringing the bell which is sounded every night to signify the closing of the market, when I locked up the shop. As a matter of fact, I attend a masonic lodge in the West End of the city and last night was our monthly meeting night. I collected my overcoat and the case containing my masonic regalia and made my way straight out on to Grainger Street where I met my fellow-mason Mr. David Conlon. We had arranged to share a taxi to the Lodge as we do every meeting night.'

Here was another coincidence. Davy Conlon was the husband of Pauline and he was known to Harry and Bob as the main street bookie in the town centre who had a deserved reputation as a somewhat unsavoury character.

'Mr Simpson, I hope you will forgive me for saying so,' Harry continued, 'but you are not typical of the people who work here in the market. For instance, you speak like a well-educated man and if you have an accent at all, it is not from these parts. In addition, your bearing and dress are not what I would have expected to see.'

'Well observed, Sergeant' was the calm response. Simpson was controlled and confident without being forthright and he seemed relaxed as he answered Harry's questions. He gave the impression he was in charge of the interview.

'Perhaps I should explain. I was born and raised in London; in Plumstead to be specific. My family was Jewish, and we had connections with the jewellery trade. When I left school, I was taken on as an apprentice cutter of diamonds and other precious stones in Hatton Garden which is the centre of the jewellery trade, and eventually I became a fully qualified cutter. It is a very specialised occupation and I was doing well when I met a girl from Newcastle and fell in love with her. You know how it is, Sergeant.

'We were married, and I moved up North; my family were not especially approving I have to say. I had enjoyed an excellent training and my prospects were very good. They had high hopes for me but, as the saying goes, love conquers all. I took out a long-term lease on the premises I have here in the market and fortunately I was well connected in the trade. I introduced myself to Joshua Mickler and Samuel Goldberg and they commissioned me to carry out occasional alterations to diamonds and other stones. This requires a level of expertise I possess, and they do not. It allows me to keep my hand in as well as supplementing my income, for which I am grateful.'

'That's fascinating, Mr. Simpson,' said Harry, genuinely impressed, 'you have a very interesting job if you don't mind me saying so. However, if I can just take you back to last night, did you happen to see anyone else as you were leaving the market?'

'I am afraid not, Sergeant. As I said, my priority was getting to the taxi rank to meet Mr. Conlon.'

'Well, thank you for your time and help. I will just ask you to write and sign your statement. The constable will look after you then you can go. If you do think of anything which you think might be useful to our enquiry, please let us know.'

Simpson completed the formalities, promising to keep in touch with the police and to contact them if he remembered anything that he thought might be relevant. Bob showed him out and he made his way back across the Alley to his shop.

'Well, he was an interesting character, to say the least, Bob.'

'He certainly was. Reticent and quietly spoken, comfortable in the limelight. Probably went to public school, judging by the way he talks and dresses and the way he carries himself. They seem to have an inner confidence, those people. It should be easy enough to check his alibi with the taxi people or Conlon. I think it would be worth having a chat with Conlon, anyway, bearing in mind his missus being so closely involved in the case. What do you reckon about these freemasons then, Guv?'

'No strong feelings really. I don't know a great deal about them to be honest. You hear rumours about them helping each other in business and I know one or two of the lads on the force are members, but I haven't been approached to join and I wouldn't really be interested. What about you?'

Bob, taking time to gather his thoughts as he normally did, said;

'My brother John at home in Glasgow is a member. He spoke to me a couple of times about joining and I was quite interested, but then I came down here and it didn't happen.'

'What was the attraction, then?'

'Well, John is a decent and civilised man and I respect him. There was also the fact that they have a very good reputation for giving to charity. The social life is also very pleasant apparently. Ena would certainly enjoy the ladies' nights. Maybe I will think about it again at some stage, but at the moment the job is my priority to be honest.'

Following his conversation with the police and subsequent statement, Israel Simpson returned straight away to his shop. He opened up the premises and made straight for the safe in the small back room. He took out two small, individual jewellers' ring cases, checked the contents carefully and placed them in a trouser pocket. He then locked the shop and made his way across the market and up the stairs to Mickler and Goldberg's Jewellery Store.

Without pausing, he went inside. Samuel Goldberg was in attendance, though there were no customers present apart from a young man who was perusing a tray of gentlemen's signet rings while carrying out an earnest conversation with Betty Forster. Simpson nodded in the direction of the back shop, where the two of them found Joshua Mickler drinking tea. Simpson came straight to the point;

'Gentlemen, there has been a development,' he announced, 'Apparently, a girl from the flower shop beside my unit was murdered last night; stabbed to death. The police have been speaking to anyone who might have seen anything suspicious. I was working on your ring and left late. I have therefore given them a statement.'

Mickler and Goldberg frowned;

'Why didn't you just keep quiet?' Samuel Goldberg demanded.

'Well, I had nothing to hide. Besides I didn't want to be in a position where I was later found to be lying to them, so I thought it was best to be up front. It was not an issue, as it was my masonic night. That was the reason I was working late as a matter of fact. I always meet up with Mr. Conlon on lodge night and we share a taxi from the town to the West End. It made sense to work a little later and finish the work on your ring, then meet up with Conlon at the taxi rank. Old Mr Hoult, the shoemaker, was there making a statement as well.'

Suitably mollified, Mickler and Goldberg turned to more pressing matters;

'What about the ring? Is it finished?' demanded Joshua Mickler.

By way of reply, Simpson reached into his right-hand trouser pocket and produced the two ring cases. He handed them to Mickler who took his magnifying glass from his pocket and studied the stones with meticulous care before pronouncing;

'The usual outstanding work, Israel. First class. Well done.'

Goldberg then crossed the room and opened the safe. He took out a bulky brown paper envelope and handed it to Simpson who tucked it into his trouser pocket without comment. His payment duly received, the men each shook Simpson's hand and he made his way back to his shop to continue his afternoon's work.

The two detectives had reached a point where they were going to learn no more on the first day of the enquiry. It was now a matter of evaluating what they had and laying out their plans for the next day. Although they were now technically off duty, they agreed to have a break, go home for their tea and meet later in the pub at the bottom of Bulmer Street.

It was just after seven o'clock when Harry Maguire stepped into the Ordnance Arms. As he had expected, Bob was sitting on an unobtrusive seat near the corner of the bar counter. He had already anticipated Harry's preference, and ordered a couple of pints of Deucher's draught ale.

The Ordnance was not a large pub, nor did it have any

pretensions. Nevertheless, it was a popular watering hole which stood on the corner of Gallowgate and Bulmer Street. It was the perfect local for Harry and Bob who lived virtually on the doorstep. It's greatest virtue and the reason for its popularity was the fact that, unusually, it did not possess a cellar for storing the beer. Instead, the casks were stood on concrete flagstones behind the serving hatch. The landlord would draw the glasses of ale and bring them up three steps to the counter.

The casks were covered by damp cloths to maintain the right temperature and this method of serving the beer 'from the wood' was much favoured by aficionados of good ale. The common perception was that beer which was kept and presented in this way was better conditioned and flavoured than beer drawn from a cellar. Mutual 'cheers' were exchanged. Bob produced his notebook and the business of the evening was at hand;

'Let's start with the victim. The location of the body suggests it was placed there but she was probably not killed there. She was carried or dragged from somewhere, possibly wrapped in a sheet or blanket and placed there for some reason possibly to delay the discovery of her body until the shop was opened this morning. Maybe that would account for the lack of blood or maybe she was stabbed in the back. The Conlon woman's statement is very helpful in terms of what she told us about Mary, but she was not really able to tell us very much about the actual crime apart from having found the body. In fairness, she stood up very well, but it doesn't take us far.'

'I agree,' replied Harry Maguire, 'and I am not sure we

learned very much from either Raymond Hoult or Israel Simpson. Hoult is an unlikely suspect due to his mobility problems. Besides, he did not see anything untoward or anyone in the vicinity of the scene of crime. Plus, his apprentice confirms their alibis. I can't imagine they were both involved. Simpson is a more complicated case and he could be worth keeping an eye on. However, he seemed relaxed enough and his alibi will be easily checked. I think it would be worthwhile having a word with Davy Conlon as well. He was apparently in the vicinity last night to meet Israel Simpson ahead of their lodge meeting. He could have been hanging around his wife's shop. At the very least we can get him to confirm Simpson's alibi. I assume you agree that Raymond Hoult is completely above suspicion?'

'No doubt is there?' Bob agreed.

'Okay, let's scratch him. What about Simpson?'

'I think he is much more interesting. The masonic get-together seems on the face of it to put both him and Conlon in the clear, but what I do think would be more useful would be to pay a visit to Mickler and Goldberg. Apart from Simpson doing specialist work for them, Betty Forster and Gordon Hugill are both employed there according to Pauline Conlon. It could be worth our while finding out what kind of set-up it is.'

'Agreed. Let's just have another look at the Conlon woman's statement, then we will be ready to outline our plans for tomorrow to the Chief Super.'

The pair sipped their beer as they read the document, then Bob said;

'Well, Guv I think she came across very well. She obviously

had a high regard for the girl and the only loose strand is her dislike of Danny Veitch. It's almost paranoid. It would be interesting to know if there is any previous between them.

'Otherwise, we should speak to Veitch. I'm looking forward to meeting that young man. The crucial thing, though, will be the post-mortem. All we know about Mary so far is that she was stabbed to death and left in a chair in the florist's shop.

'Hopefully, George Howes will be able to give us a whole lot of background which will give a firm line of enquiry to follow. I'll keep a record of what he has to say and we should have a copy of his report fairly quickly.

'We'll need to speak to Betty Forster as well,' Harry said, 'to get some more background on Mary. That should give us plenty to keep us going.'

'What about Gordon Hugill?'

'We can leave him until we have spoken to Betty. We also need a statement from Davy Conlon. He may have seen someone acting suspiciously or have been up to no good himself. Either way we need to speak to him. The most important person we speak to could be Danny Veitch. He was going out with the victim. He was meant to meet her at the Oxford. We need to know if he turned up and if so whether or not he carries a knife which is certainly rumoured.'

'Right,' said Harry, 'so that's the post-mortem, Betty Forster, Davy Conlon, Danny Veitch and possibly Hugill, and the jewellers. That should give us a lot more to get our teeth into. We won't be in the Grainger Market, and PC Lloyd will be based in the police station. He will be arranging the interviews and co-ordinating things in general. PC Doyle can keep an eye on the shop and the temporary Incident Room. We might get some more reaction from our request for late workers who saw anything suspicious and there is always the possibility of somebody having remembered something.

'We'll recommend to Chief Superintendent Walton that we close the Incident Room in the Market after tomorrow and move the whole operation back to the station. We can let Mrs. Conlon re-open her shop. There is no reason for it to stay closed and the poor woman has a business to run. She seems the determined type who would rather be busy in these circumstances than sitting around at home and moping. We'll meet up for work as usual and when we arrive at the station, we will make the Chief Super's office our first port of call.'

With that, they drained their glasses, took their leave of the pub landlord and made their way up Bulmer Street to their respective homes, pausing only to lament the fact that Varley's Fish and Chip shop, which adjoined the Ordnance and was just as revered it its own way for the quality of the product it offered, was regrettably closed. Some of their admirable fish and chips wrapped in newspaper would have rounded their first day on the case perfectly.

They had not made much tangible progress as far as solving the crime was concerned, but at least they now had a feel for the case. They were properly focussed, and both felt that tomorrow should be considerably more interesting.

CHAPTER FOUR

WEDNESDAY, 3RD OCTOBER

DS HARRY Maguire and DC Bob Frame had a busy day in prospect. They met as usual at 7:30 at the bottom of Bulmer Street. Neither man's mood was improved by the unpleasant, penetrating drizzle which fell from the lowering sky.

'Gloomy day again, Harry.'

'Pretty grim, but we will be indoors all day, so once we get to the station we should be protected from the elements.'

The two police officers set off, coat collars turned up against the weather, on the walk down Darn Crook into the town centre to the city police station on Market Street. It was their preferred route, which they varied occasionally to go down Blackett Street if the mood took them. Bob stifled a groan as Harry embarked on the history lesson he always delivered at this point;

'Did I ever tell you this was a cul-de-sac blocked off by the old town wall which was breached by marauding Scots in 16-something?'

'No offence, Guv, but you tell me nearly every time we take this route!'

Harry took the dig in good spirit;

'1644 actually. Just shows how much notice you take. I need to keep telling you if I'm to make a proper Geordie out of you.' Bob rolled his eyes and prepared himself for the full history of the street whose name meant 'a dark and secret place.'

A briefing with their boss, Chief Superintendent Walton, was the first item on Harry and Bob's agenda after a hot cup of tea in the staff canteen. The Spectre seemed satisfied with a quick resume of the previous day's activities and an outline of what promised to be a busy schedule, including the post-mortem on the victim and a list of the people due in for interview. They made their way to the Incident Room where PC Lloyd handed them an official list of the day's activities. The inquest was at 10:30 and on their instructions, Lloyd had arranged the remaining witness interviews with the appropriate people at sensible intervals throughout the rest of the day;

'We have Betty Forster and her parents coming in at 1:30, Sergeant,' Lloyd advised them, 'and during the afternoon Danny Veitch and Mr. Conlon, the bookmaker, are due to make statements.'

'Good work, Constable. You stay here and keep an eye on matters, and we will be back after the post-mortem to see the Forsters.'

PC Doyle, meanwhile, was handed the keys of the Incident Room in the market with instructions to make himself available in case anyone else turned up having remembered something from the night of the crime.

A post-mortem examination was obligatory when a violent or unexplained death took place. The post-mortem on Mary Bartlett was to be conducted in the mortuary; an integral facility of the new Market Street Police Station, by George Howes, the highly respected police surgeon who carried out all such examinations for the city force.

Harry and Bob were required to attend as investigating officers and they stood in the viewing gallery as George dissected the body and delivered his findings. Bob Frame listened with fixed concentration, setting down any factors he regarded as significant. He would be further advised by a later examination of the written post-mortem report. This document would be forwarded to the Incident Room and placed in the case file.

George began in a clear, objective tone;

'The deceased is a female aged 23 years and her death was caused by a single stab wound which was inflicted by an 8-inch butcher's steak knife. There is evidence of bleeding as a result of the knife having entered through the left aorta from the back with considerable force. There was no sign of blood in the vicinity of the location where the body was found. This would suggest that some form of sheet or blanket was used to wrap the body to prevent blood falling to the ground.

'There is an external bruise to the forehead and grazing to the left knee which indicate that prior to her death the victim suffered a significant fall. It is not possible to determine whether the fall was as a trip or slip on her part or as a result of a push from behind by an assailant, but it is extremely likely the fall was caused by one of these means.

'It is possible that as a result of the fall the victim lost consciousness for a short period of time prior to her death.

She would, in all probability, have been in a groggy and semi-conscious state immediately afterwards. There is no evidence to suggest she attempted to defend herself from attack at any time.

'An examination of the contents of the stomach reveals an absence of alcohol. There is evidence of the victim having eaten a small quantity of plain biscuits and consumed half a pint of water. The removal of pelvic organs, bladder, uterus and ovaries shows she did not suffer any form of sexual attack. Nor was she pregnant.

'Materials found on the periphery of the abrasions to the forehead and knee are consistent with those found on the floor of the Grainger Market is constructed suggesting her fall was sustained in that location. This view is reinforced by the presence in the wounds of specks of sawdust, which is routinely thrown on the floor of the market by butchers when they are cutting the carcases of beasts.

'The determination of the time of death does not normally fall within the remit of the post-mortem examination except where there is demonstrable evidence. In this case, it is known that the victim was dead when the owner of the florist's shop opened the premises at 7:30 am. There is no witness or confirming evidence as to the time of death beyond the fact that the victim was alive when the shop owner saw her at 5:00 pm the previous evening.

'In conclusion, the bruising and grazing on the victim's body is almost certainly a result of a fall on the Grainger Market floor. Her body was then removed from that location and placed on a chair inside Conlon's Florist's where it was subsequently found by the owner of the shop, Mrs. Pauline

Conlon. It is my summation, based on the evidence at my disposal, that Mary Bartlett lost her life as a result of a single knife wound to the heart, inflicted by person or persons unknown.

'Howes said he would forward a copy of his findings to the Incident Room where it could be placed in the murder file. No sooner had George Howes finished delivering his post-mortem verdict than Harry Maguire and Bob Frame sought him out to pick his brains further if they could.

'Your usual thorough and precise work, George. Most helpful, thanks,' Harry said. There is no doubt that there is any blood on the market floor in the vicinity?'

'Afraid not, Harry. I know it would help you if there were and I had that in mind when I was examining the floor, but there was none, I assure you.'

'Just one more thing, if you don't mind. This cloth or sheet which was used to absorb any bleeding. Does that imply that perhaps there was more than one person involved?'

'You know I don't like speculating, Harry. I deal in facts. All I can suggest is that it is a possibility. I know where you are going with the question in terms of impulse or pre-meditation, but there is no evidence to confirm whether the body was moved by one person or two I'm afraid.'

Harry thanked George for his off the record opinion and he and Bob returned to the Incident Room to carry out their analysis of his findings. Bob led the discussion, referring to his own supplementary notes.

'Some of the information is on the fringe of our investigation and we can dismiss it. The stomach contents, for instance, tell us nothing and the fact that Mary was not pregnant is not a surprise. We know already she died of a single stab wound but we did not know there was no other external bleeding, which is useful. There are plenty of butchers' steak knives in the market, though that could quite easily be a red herring.

'Let's look at the rest of the information and see where that takes us. The external bruising is probably the most important clue. As George said, she obviously fell heavily and bruised her forehead and knee. The question is, was her fall as a result as a trip from running. If so, was she running away from someone or simply hurrying to get to the dance? Either way, it must have been a hefty fall if it could have caused to her knock herself out.

'George seemed convinced the bruising was caused by her falling on the market floor, so she lay there in the open, possibly unconscious, and most likely in no condition to defend herself. We think Pauline Conlon was the last person to see her alive at about 5:00 o'clock. When she opened the shop next morning and found the body, the wreaths Mary had stayed behind to complete were finished which narrows our window somewhat.

'If we assume the work took her about three quarters of an hour to finish, that would mean she was still alive at 5:45. It seems unlikely there would still be more than one or two stragglers in the market at that time. The closing bell is rung officially at six. The bulk of the stalls and shops actually close at 5:00 or 5:30. If we are right in our calculation that she was alive at 5:45, it would take next to no time for her to put on her coat, lock the shop door and make her way towards the market exit. If we then take into account her fall, we have a very narrow time scale in which she was killed.

'The Market Superintendent would be in the process of locking the doors, and opportunities for leaving the market would be extremely limited for anyone trying to make a getaway. We can assume for the moment that the Superintendent was not involved, though we will need to confirm his movements to be on the safe side.

'She was defenceless when she was attacked, and her stabbed body was carried from where she was killed and placed in the shop. Presumably, she was moved so that it would not be possible to determine the actual location where she was attacked. The shop was chosen because it was close at hand, which presumes the killer either knew she worked there or saw her rushing from the premises before she fell. Maybe he rifled her pockets and found the shop keys which gave him access.

'All of this took place in a relatively short period of time and it does not give us any real idea of why it happened. It was either a random killing, which I personally doubt – why hide the body and risk being seen, instead of simply running away?–or, it was deliberate in which case what was the motive? Had she seen something or someone she should not have seen? That seems to me to be the likeliest reason. Was she simply in the wrong place at the wrong time? Why would someone stab a young woman in the back who was lying on the floor recovering from a hefty fall? A normal person's instinct would be to stop and help. There are more questions than answers. We have plenty to go on, but we are still really in the dark about why she was killed. Do you have any theories, Guv?'

Harry had been troubled by the same problem: lack of motive;

'My instinct is that it was not random. She had either been followed from the shop and, when she fell, her assailant saw an opportunity to kill her, or the killer saw her lying on the market floor unconscious and he stabbed her there. Either way, it is hard to figure out why. Also, I do not believe robbery was the motive. She was a shop girl and was not carrying any takings or other large amounts of money.

'I would suggest we re-visit the market and try to identify the scene of crime, but it would probably be a waste of time without any bloodstains. Besides, the market is open for business and hundreds of people will have walked over the area and contaminated any potential evidence. All I know is, it must have been relatively close to the shop for the body to be transported.

'Maybe we should also consider the possibility there might have been more than one person involved in order to carry out the killing, move the body and open and close the shop before making a getaway. I am not convinced, but it is not something we can overlook.'

'Okay, where do we start?' Bob asked.

'We need to find a motive. I cannot see an obvious one, but someone killed an apparently innocent young woman and we need to presume they thought they had a good reason. If we can work out what that reason was, we could be on our way to catching the killer.'

CHAPTER FIVE

WEDNESDAY, 3RD OCTOBER

FOLLOWING THE post-mortem, Harry and Bob decided to go back to the Grainger Market to speak to the Market Superintendent. They needed to ask him about his movements the previous night. It was an exercise in removing his name from any list of suspects and it would be an expedient way of filling the time until they had to interview Betty Forster.

The Superintendent was a little sheepish when Harry asked him politely about the previous night, though it was made clear he was not under suspicion.

'Let me be honest, Sergeant, and tell you I was not alone as I rang the bell and did my round of locking the gates. It was my wedding anniversary yesterday, as chance happens, and my wife and I had arranged to go for a drink when I finished work by way of celebration. She met me here and walked around with me as I locked up, then we made our way together to the Adelphi pub on Shakespeare Street. We bumped into a couple of the market people on the way if that helps.

'We were there by about quarter past six. Jimmy, the landlord, gave us a drink on the house when I told him it was our anniversary. I didn't see or hear anybody as I was locking up, I'm afraid.'

That seemed to Harry and Bob to be a fairly tight alibi, which was no more than they had expected. The people the Superintendent had identified as seeing on the way to the Adelphi would be easily tracked down in order to confirm his story. As they had anticipated, they had time to grab a quick sandwich from the canteen before they returned to the Incident Room when they arrived back at the police station. At just before 12:30, DS Maguire and DS Frame were primed and ready to interview Betty Forster in the presence of her parents. They had been taken aback when Mr. Forster had asked if he and his wife could accompany Betty and be present when she was spoken to. This was normally the practice when a child or a juvenile was interviewed, but it was extremely rare when an adult like Betty Forster was involved.

However, Mr. Forster's request was based on his belief that while Mary actually had a job which brought her into daily contact with the general public, she was nevertheless nervous and reticent in unfamiliar surroundings, especially where authoritarian figures like the police were involved.

'It will be a massive ordeal for her, Sergeant, but she wants to give you as much help as she can. She will be fine when she settles. She was Mary's best friend, after all, and this business has devastated her. She will have no problems if her mother and I are there. We just need to be in the room. We'll keep quiet. We won't interfere. We don't need to hold her hand or anything like that.'

Harry could see where Mr. Forster was coming from, but

he still needed convincing;

'Betty is 25 years old and she has held down a responsible job for several years. She is in daily contact with the public. If she was tongue tied dealing with the customers in the jeweller's, surely she would not have lasted long.'

'That is different, Mr. Maguire. She loves her work and, somehow, she comes alive when she is in the shop. She doesn't feel threatened and she is quite happy dealing with the public. I know it sounds peculiar, but all Betty wants is what is best for Mary and she thinks our being there will relax her.'

'Okay, Mr. Forster. I am willing to accept your request, but I must impose some conditions; legal constraints if you like. As well as being unobtrusive you must not speak or attempt to prompt or communicate with Betty in any way. If either of you should do so I would have to ask you to leave the room.'

Harry had reservations but he wanted the interview to provide any information Betty might have. The Forster's seemed a decent couple so in the end he saw no compelling reason why they should not be present providing they abided by his guidelines. He believed that it was in the interests of the police as well as Betty that she could feel comfortable and able to provide any information she might have. The Forster family were ushered into the interview room by Bob Frame;

'Mr. and Mrs. Forster, thank you for coming. If you could just sit over there please,' he pointed to a couple of seats located against the wall and outside of Betty's line of vision. He then took Betty to a seat facing Harry's desk before returning to sit alongside her parents.

Harry began the interview in an informal way to try and create a relaxing atmosphere;

'Hello Betty. My name is Harry Maguire and my colleague is called Bob Frame. We are the officers in charge of the investigation into Mary's very sad death. We would like to ask you a few questions so we can get to know Mary better. I know this is a huge ordeal for you, but you would be helping us a great deal. Are you all right with that?'

At first appearance Betty gave the impression of being a timid young woman and she turned out to be quietly spoken. Initial impressions suggested she was not a worldly girl and possibly was naïve, but this in no way implied a lack of intelligence. She was small of stature and quite pleasant in appearance without being beautiful or striking and her most distinguishing features were her sparkling eyes, and attractive, well-groomed blonde hair.

'I'll try, sir.'

'Good. Now, I understand you and Mary were best friends. Is that right?'

'Yes, sir.'

'I know how upsetting this is for you, but the more we learn about Mary, the quicker we can find out who was responsible. How did you come to know Mary, Betty?'

'We were in the same class at school, sir. We shared a desk.'

Betty was speaking quietly and appeared a little uncomfortable in the situation, but she seemed to be un-phased under Harry's sympathetic initial questioning. His friendly tone was designed to help her relax and he hoped the fact that he had rather reluctantly agreed to her father's request for the parents to be present at the interview would prove helpful. He was intent on giving her the confidence that she was in no way a suspect, but simply someone who could help the investigation. Although uneasy in the situation, she was doing her best to be helpful. He perceived her as a bright girl who, with careful handling, would give a good account of herself.

'And when you left school you both got jobs in the Grainger Market?'

'Yes, sir. Mary started with Mrs. Conlon in the flower shop and I got a job in the jewellers on the other side of the market.'

'Did Mary like her job, do you think? 'Oh yes, sir, she loved it. She really enjoyed working with the flowers and doing wedding bouquets and funeral wreaths. She said Mrs. Conlon was strict, but she could also be kind and she liked working for her.

'Harry was anxious to learn as much as he could about Mary Bartlett, but he was also anxious to assess Betty Forster's credibility as a potential witness, so he switched his line of questioning and settled on asking Betty about herself, hoping her growing confidence and relaxation would encourage her to be more forthcoming.

'What about you, Betty. Do you like your job?'

'Definitely, sir. It's really nice. I get to show the customers the trays of rings. I help them to choose. Sometimes rings, sometimes necklaces or earrings. I love the colours and designs and you get to meet some very friendly people.'

'Do the owners of the jewellery shop treat you well?

'Certainly. Mr. Joshua and Mr. Samuel are really kind.

Mr. Samuel is quite funny and tells jokes, and Mr Joshua is more serious, but they are both friendly.'

'I understand you have a boyfriend who works their as well. Is that right?'

Betty blushed and twisted her hands. She looked at the floor before answering.

'Yes, Mr. Maguire. His name is Gordon Hugill. He is training in the workshop and he sometimes helps Mr. Simpson doing repairs and fitting stones. He can't work on the shop counter because he stammers, but he is very clever.'

'Would you say it was serious between you?'

Betty considered the question carefully before answering.

'Quite serious, I suppose. We have been going out for six months now. We are both quiet, Mr. Maguire, and I suppose we suit each other.'

'Was Mary quiet, too, Betty. Did she ever lose her temper?'

'No, she wasn't as quiet as me, but she wasn't boisterous or anything like that. She could stick up for herself if she needed to. She liked a laugh, but she certainly wasn't flighty or common. Mary was a respectable girl. She went to church with her mam every Sunday.'

'You are doing really well, Betty. Now, I want you to tell me about Tuesday night. Some of you were going dancing at the Oxford Galleries in town. Is that correct?'

Betty brightened considerably at this new line of questioning. She appeared to be perfectly relaxed and even possibly enjoying the experience now that she was content that she was not feeling threatened in any way.

'That's right. There was me and Mary, then there was Norma who works in the chemist's and Lorraine. Her mam and dad have a fruit and veg stall and she helps out on that. Mary was working late because they had a big funeral and she said she would see us there.'

'Were you worried when she didn't turn up?' 'Not really. I just thought she might have been held up or maybe she was tired after work and decided to go straight home. It's quite demanding work she does and sometimes she would say she was tired at the end of the day.'

'What about your boyfriends? Were they both at the dance?'

'Yes, but they were both late. They had been for a pint on the way. Danny said he had been to the Three Bulls and Gordon reckoned he had been in the Eldon. To be honest, Mr. Maguire, neither of them are very keen on dancing. They probably went to the pub to pick up some Dutch courage. Neither of them is a big drinker. I couldn't be doing with that, but a pint of beer now and again never did anyone any harm, did it?'

This was a sentiment with which Harry heartily concurred. He was beginning to warm to Betty Forster!

'How often does the group of you go dancing at the Oxford, Betty?'

'Usually twice a week. Nearly every Tuesday and also we go on a Saturday night.'

'Was Mary one of the regulars?'

'Oh, yes. She loved dancing. Actually, the two of us quite often danced together. It was good fun. The lads would get up from time to time, but the girls all loved dancing and we would dance together with our handbags at our feet for safe keeping. Well, you couldn't expect the boyfriends to hold them, could you?'

For the first time in their conversation Betty allowed herself a small, self-deprecating laugh which Harry countered with a pleasant smile. This interview was going better than he could have hoped. Perhaps, though, the hardest part came now, as he introduced the subject of Danny Veitch into the conversation;

'Would you say Mary had fallen out or quarrelled with anyone recently?'

Betty's reply was quite animated;

'Oh no, sir. Mary didn't get into arguments. She was too nice. She was going out with Danny and she seemed very happy.'

'What about Danny? Do you like him?'

'I don't really know him very well. They had only just started going out together. I know he works at one of the butchers in the market, but I work on the other side and I don't see him very often. He seems all right, though, and he was good to Mary.'

'Betty, you have been really helpful,' Harry said as he drew the interview to a conclusion.' We will be trying our very best to find out what happened to your friend, I promise you. Thank you for coming in. If you think of anything else perhaps you could tell your Mam and Dad and come in again to talk to us.'

Harry turned to Betty's parents;

'Mr. and Mrs. Forster, thank you for your help. Betty has been very brave. We will need her to sign a written statement at some stage, but that can wait.'

As Betty and her parents prepared to leave, there was a

knock on the door and a young man of unprepossessing appearance entered the room. He turned out to be Gordon Hugill, who had come to take Betty back to work. He wore a suit in which he looked uncomfortable and a tie with which he constantly fidgeted. He was clearly ill at ease and when Harry reached across to shake his hand and said;

'How do you do Gordon?'

He looked at the floor and mumbled barely audibly; 'H-h-h-how do you d-d-do,sir.'

Harry and Bob were delighted with the interview. Not only had Betty provided some useful background information on the dead woman, but she had proven herself to be a young lady with a lot more about her than they had been led to expect by her father. She had also expressed useful opinions on both Gordon Hugill and Danny Veitch, and even given them a small insight into life at Mickler and Goldberg's. This was useful stuff and went way beyond what they had anticipated.

Encouraged by the information they had received from Mary's friend, Betty, the officers were keen to get on with the other interviews they had scheduled for the day. Still on their list were Davy Conlon and Danny Veitch, so they instructed PC Lloyd to show Conlon into the interview room.

If Betty had turned out to be much more than the shrinking violet they had expected, their instincts told them that Mr. Conlon would be considerably more predictable.

Although changes had just this year been made to the laws regarding gambling under the 1934 Betting and Gambling Act, they applied principally to on-course betting. The new law was aimed at controlling the number of race meetings which could take place on a given registered racecourse, with the aim of restricting on-course betting. No mention was made of street gambling. The Act had not addressed the issue of working-class men who liked a flutter, but in the main placed modest bets with a street bookmaker.

Going to the races was very much a pursuit of the middle and wealthy classes and was beyond the pockets of artisans. The laws as they stood with regard to street gambling were fundamentally inadequate and in practice virtually unenforceable. While street gambling was technically against the law, the police tended to take an ambivalent view. This meant that people like Conlon and his kind were wealthy men. They would be arrested periodically and brought before the magistrates, but the outcome was invariably a nominal fine and a gentle tap on the knuckles. The so-called offenders would feign contrition and then return to the streets to continue in their very lucrative ways.

David Francis Conlon looked the part. He was a large man, florid of face with a whisky drinker's nose and a greedy man's stomach. He was neither handsome nor attractive, but nevertheless regarded himself as a man about town. He was a ladies' man whose money and his willingness to spend it on the opposite sex meant he was never short of amenable companions whose morals coincided with his own.

He wore the best of clothes; a Crombie overcoat with a fashionable velvet collar, and hand-made calf boots. His shirts were silk and obtained from Jermyn Street, as were his ties. He invariably sported an expensive cigar. He was a familiar figure in the town centre, and he was known to

Harry and Bob in their professional capacity in a superficial way. Neither of them held him in high regard.

Conlon owned a flat in Leazes Park Road which by his own admission he used as the base for his extra-marital activities. All-in-all, beneath his smooth veneer, he was a sleazy individual whose money was his passport to what he regarded as good living.

Maguire invited him to sit down, then began the interview;

'As you will realise, Mr, Conlon, we are talking to anyone who might have been in the vicinity of your wife's premises last night or had any connection with the victim, so I need you to give us an account of your movements in the period leading up to the crime.'

Conlon was relaxed, confident and almost supercilious as he began his response;

'Certainly. Happy to oblige. I was in town in the afternoon paying takings into the bank then, at about four o'clock, possibly quarter past, I went to Carrick's cafe on Grey Street for tea. I go there quite often. I was sitting beside what they call the 'jewellers' table where the Jewish jewellers meet every afternoon to deal in their private collections away from their shops. They are there every day, as I say, and I can tell you the sums of money that change hands would make your mouth water.

This was true. They had their premises where they conducted their retail business but these supplementary meetings were for inter-jeweller trading which might involve the re-distribution–at a profit–of large amounts of gold and jewellery brought into the country by refugees seeking to sell some of their savings in order to set up in business in the United Kingdom.

'Anyway, I had my tea, then I smoked a cigar and by then it was about five. It was my monthly masonic meeting night. I usually meet Israel Simpson, the jobbing jeweller who has a shop close to my wife's, and we share a taxi to the lodge on Maple Terrace in the West End.

'I was a bit early, so I had a whisky in the Bacchus beside the Theatre Royal, then I walked up to the taxi rank near Grey's Monument and met Simpson who had arrived just before me.'

Conlon's outline of his afternoon's activities, though brief, seemed eminently plausible and it would surely be easy enough to verify if necessary, as he was a flamboyant and instantly recognisable character in the city centre.

Nevertheless, Harry put the question;

'Can anyone verify any of this? Did you speak to anyone in the Bacchus, for instance?'

'I can't think of anyone specific, but I would be surprised if you couldn't find someone,' replied Conlon with a raised eyebrow.

As things stood, Israel Simpson and Davy Conlon appeared to have provided each other with alibis for at least a part of the period during which Mary Bartlett was murdered. For the moment both gentlemen were regarded of little interest, to be returned to if the situation demanded. Harry had no supplementary questions at that stage, so he and Bob thanked Conlon for his time. He wrote and signed his statement then he left the station.

This left them with one final interview for the day: Danny

Veitch, the recently acquired boyfriend of the deceased and a young man who had managed to incur the disapproval of Pauline Conlon.

'We've got twenty minutes before Veitch. See if you can sweet talk Doyle into bringing us a brew can you, Bob?'

'Excellent idea, Guv.'

Bob pushed himself out of his chair and stuck his head out of the door to pass on Harry's instructions.

'So, what do we know about Veitch, then, apart from Pauline Conlon's aspersions about him bring handy with a knife?'

Bob lifted a page from Mary Bartlett's file and read aloud;

'Daniel Arthur Veitch. 24 year old butcher employed by Huddlestone's in the Grainger Market. Tall and well-built with copper coloured hair. Hearsay evidence that he is good at his job. Rumoured to carry a knife routinely, but no record of him having been involved in any violence. No dealings with the police. Summoned to Market Street Police Station for questioning as current boyfriend of deceased Mary Bartlett. Subject of alleged character shortcomings in statement by Pauline Conlon.'

'That's it Guv. Short and sweet. Clean sheet and good at his job, but some reservations.'

'Mm…time to wheel him in and find out for ourselves. We've only got the conflicting opinions of Pauline Conlon and Betty Forster to go on. Bring him in, Bob.'

The young man who was shown in by PC Doyle was of striking appearance and seemed to be relaxed. His image matched the reputation he had among his peers as self-confident to a point close to arrogance. Those who knew him best, though, would tell you that his somewhat brash exterior disguised a less self-absorbed and insular inner self. It would be interesting to see how he handled himself.

The Veitch family lived in Leazes Lane in the town centre. Mr. Veitch was employed as a casual labourer on the quayside and Danny had an older sister who worked as an auxiliary nurse in the Royal Victoria Infirmary which was situated a literal stone's throw from the Veitch residence. His mother, Mrs. Veitch, was the matriarch who bonded the family together. She held down two jobs. As well as being a cleaner at St. Andrew's Church of England School, just around the corner, she was the caretaker of St. Andrew's Church Hall on Leazes Park Road. She was regarded as a diligent and reliable employee who brooked no nonsense and who was a strong character.

The school and the church hall had always been administered by the elders of St. Andrew's Church located on the corner of Newgate Street and Darn Crook. The church lays claim, with ample justification, to be the oldest place of worship in Newcastle.

Despite his reputation, neither Maguire or Frame, nor indeed any of the officers at Market Street, had occasion to come in to contact with Veitch. The only line of form they had was the rather tenuous one included in Pauline Conlon's statement, in which she admitted and antipathy towards him. The comments of Betty Forster had been positive, though neither woman knew him well enough for their opinions to be definitive. It was time for the two detectives to form their own opinions.

'Danny, this is a bad business and we need to talk to

you about your relationship with Mary Bartlett,' said Harry Maguire by way of an opening gambit. 'We also need you to account for your movements on Tuesday night. Are you all right with that?'

Danny nodded and muttered in the affirmative.

'People tell me you had been seeing Mary for just over a couple of weeks. Is that right?'

'About that, yes.'

'How did you meet?'

'I had seen her about the market from time to time and I chatted her up. I knew her from the flower shop. We went to the dance at the Oxford a couple of times and it started from there, but it hadn't become too serious. We got on well and we liked each other, but it was early days.'

'What about Tuesday night? You had arranged to meet at the dance hall?'

'Yes. I had offered to wait for her until she finished work, but she didn't know what time she would be done, so we arranged to meet at the dance hall.'

'What about you? Did you go straight there?'

'No. I went home from work and had a wash and a shave and changed into my suit. Then I walked down to Percy Street to the Three Bulls Heads. The pub is on the way from our house on Leazes Lane, so I called in for a pint because I knew Mary would be late.'

'Is there anyone who could vouch for you?'

'I'm not sure. Maybe not. I actually didn't meet anyone I knew. I just stood at the bar having a quiet drink. Maybe the barmaid would remember, but I would have to check. I left about seven and walked down to the Oxford. I saw

Mary's mate Betty as well as her boyfriend, Gordon Hugill, who works with her at the jewellers. Obviously, Mary didn't show up, but I had no idea why not. I assumed she couldn't get away or maybe she'd gone straight home. I chatted with a couple of lads from the market for a bit then I walked home.'

'You didn't call at Mary's to see if she was okay?'

'No, she lived on Stanton Street which is a canny way from our house. Mary's Mam wouldn't be worried either. She trusted Mary and usually turned in at about ten apparently.'

'What about Wednesday morning? How did you find out about Mary?'

'I got to work for about ten to nine and went for a cup of tea at one of the stalls. A couple of lads were talking about some lass being killed. When I heard them mention the flower shop, I walked down there and saw a couple of policemen hanging about. I didn't have time to find out any details of what had happened. I needed to be at work.'

'You didn't follow it up?'

'No. One of the butchers came across and mentioned it but to be honest I didn't really want to talk about it or get involved.'

'Why was that? People were telling you your girlfriend had been killed and you weren't bothered?'

'It wasn't that I wasn't bothered. To be honest, Sergeant, I have a bit of a reputation around the market and I just wanted to keep out of it.'

'What kind of a reputation would that be Danny?'

'Well, maybe I make my mouth go when I shouldn't and I get into arguments, but I am not as bad as I am painted. As a matter of fact, I have been trying to hold my tongue since I started going out with Mary. I managed pretty well because I didn't want to upset her.'

'Did you not think it would be a good idea to come and see us? Maybe ask what had happened and make sure you had an alibi? You do realise that according to your own words there is no-one who can support your account of your movements that night between Conlon's shop closing and Mary being killed? You reckon you were in the pub but didn't speak to anyone. You were not particularly bothered when Mary failed to turn up at the dance. She was your girlfriend, but you didn't take the trouble to check on her. When you realised this morning that it was Mary who had been killed, you kept your mouth shut and stayed out of the way.'

Danny's image as a tough guy was beginning to take a hammering. He was obviously being wrong-footed by Harry's line of questioning, which was showing him up in a very uncomplimentary light.'

'When you put it like that, I suppose it does seem a bit strange, but I meant nothing by it. I was worried sick that I would get the blame. It's easy to point the finger when you have a reputation, Mr, Maguire. I hadn't been seeing Mary long, but I really cared for her and I was upset, believe me. By the way, there were people who saw me and spoke to me at the dance.'

'Where you arrived late and left early. Another thing, Danny: it has been suggested to us you carry a knife and you are quite handy with it. Is that true?'

'No! I have heard that stuff but, honestly, it's nonsense. The fact is, I have my own set of work knives that cost me a lot of money. I take them home with me every night to clean them and sharpen them. Then I take them back to work the next morning. That's the only time I carry them and that is the only reason, honest.'

'Did you take them home last night?'

'Aye.'

'I will need to see them.'

'That is not a problem, Sergeant. As a matter of fact, I have then on me. I am never without them.' Danny reached behind himself into the pocket of his overcoat and produced a roll of chamois leather containing a set of butchers' knives. Harry passed the package to Bob Frame who left the room, taking the knives. He handed them over to PC Doyle with instructions to arrange for them to be examined for human blood.

'Now then, Danny. We have a situation here which does not look particularly good for you. I need to make some further enquiries and I will certainly want to speak to you again. In the meantime, I suggest you continue with your new policy of keeping your mouth shut. It might also be in your best interest to go back to the Three Bulls and find someone who saw you there on Tuesday night. At this stage I am not accusing you of anything, but I need you to work harder to provide yourself with an alibi I can believe in. Okay?'

'Okay, Sergeant.'

'I will need to keep your knives until we have completed testing them. You should be able to collect them from the desk sergeant in the morning on your way to work.'

It was a chastened and considerably less cocksure Danny

Veitch who left Market Street Police Station that afternoon than the one who had come in an hour earlier; a judgement confirmed by Bob Frame;

'You have certainly taken the wind out of that young man's sails, Harry.'

'Well, I fancy he may be more bravado than villain, but we need to confirm that he was in the Three Bulls when he said he was last night, and we need to be certain those knives of his are free from human blood. That said, he does not appear to have any motive. He had only been going out with the girl for a couple of weeks.

'He may not be particularly popular, especially with the Conlon woman, but that means nothing and there does not appear to have been any falling out between him and Mary. They had arranged to meet at the dance and although he was late, he did turn up.'

On balance, Bob Frame was inclined to agree with his boss's assessment;

'He seems to be a typical young man. Full of himself on the surface but not so brazen when the chips are down. We will never know, of course, but I wouldn't mind betting Mary would have licked him into shape. On the other hand, if no-one at the Three Bulls can verify his story, he still has questions to answer in any case. He handled himself reasonably well considering the grilling we gave him, and he is bright enough, but you would still have expected him to be more emotional about the whole business.'

It had been an intriguing afternoon which left the two detectives with plenty of food for thought. They were ambivalent in their evaluation on Danny Veitch and they had learned precious little from Davy Conlon, though Betty Forster's evidence had been much more illuminating. They had yet to assess the interviews with Davy Conlon and Betty Forster. They had also gleaned a great deal from the findings of George Howes' post-mortem that morning, and the case file was substantially thicker than it had been at the start of the day. They would not be lacking in lines of enquiry to follow up, but in all honesty, they were yet to make a significant breakthrough. They still had no idea why Mary Bartlett had been murdered nor who was responsible.

CHAPTER SIX

THURSDAY, 4TH OCTOBER

THE MORNING of day three of the Mary Bartlett murder enquiry, saw the two investigating officers, Detective Sergeant Harry Maguire and Detective Constable Bob Frame, in a rather more relaxed mood. They were not expecting quite the same level of intensity as the last couple of days had brought. At 7:30 sharp Bob Frame drew on his first cigarette of the day; gazing approvingly at a cloudless sky and hoping it signalled the end of the dismal weather. Harry's approaching footsteps seemed to Bob to have a jauntiness which had been missing previously and his boss was whistling the upbeat 'You Ought to be in Pictures' by Rudy Vallee instead of the melancholy melodies of the previous two days.

'Morning, Guv, Brighter day, eh?'

'More like the thing, Bob.'

That was it. The daily ritual of a brief assessment of the weather and off they set. This morning, they made their first port of call when they arrived at Market Street the boss's office, where they brought the Chief Superintendent up to date with developments. He nodded and made encouraging noises and sent them on their way. Walton was basically content that his decision to put Maguire and Frame in charge of a major case was, so far, proving justified.

Harry and Bob mulled over the Bartlett case over their morning mug of tea before retracing their steps back to Gallowgate to carry out the straightforward task of taking Tommy Patterson's routine statement. It was in order to complete two of the wreaths for the funeral of Tommy's wife that Mary Bartlett stayed late on the night of her murder. While Tommy was obviously not a suspect it was necessary to speak to him as he had come into recent contact with the victim.

Tommy owned a newsagent's shop which was on the route the two detectives sometimes took to work. He was not always open when they passed, but they would call in occasionally if either them had run out of cigarettes, though they were not particularly frequent customers and their relationship with the owner was a casual one. However, the shop would definitely be open for business by now and it made sense to get a minor chore out of the way.

Being located in the shadow of St James' Park, the home of Newcastle United Football Club, it was no surprise that some of the Newcastle players made it an almost daily ritual to call at Patterson's after training for a cooling soft drink and a chat, and such was the case as Harry and Bob called in on their visit that morning to take Tommy's statement.

The small group standing at the end of the counter sipping drinks and chatting included Sammy Weaver, Newcastle's star player and club captain. Also in attendance was Tommy Pearson, a Scotsman who had signed from Murrayfield Amateurs at the start of the season. This particular morning the group was completed by the Newcastle goalkeeper, a local lad called Norman Tapken from North Shields and another of Bob's fellow countrymen, Harry McMenemy. Bob and Harry gave them a smile and a nod by way of acknowledgement.

Tommy Patterson had a clean bill of health as far as the police were concerned except when he was the unwitting subject of an unfounded claim made by a disgruntled supporter that he had been involved in the selling of players' tickets for the 1932 FA Cup Final. The allegation was quickly proven to be without foundation.

Tommy had been expecting the visit from the police in connection with the order of flowers for his wife's funeral and he made them welcome. To Harry's pleasure, not to mention Bob Frame's unparalleled delight, he introduced them to the footballers and after a few minutes of genial football chat, Tommy called his daughter from the back shop. He asked her to keep an eye on things while he wrote his statement.

He confirmed that he had placed the order for the flowers and that he had been served by Mary Bartlett. He went on to assert that he had been at home with his daughter and son-in-law all night on Tuesday. Asked by Bob if he had known Mary, he replied that he had not, but had met her twice in the process of selecting funeral flowers. He said that she seemed a very pleasant and helpful young woman who had treated him sympathetically and offered him good advice regarding the floral tributes, which he was grateful to act upon. It was Tommy's desire for a lavish funeral with an impressive floral display, augmented by floral tributes from several of his customers which had created the need for Mary to stay behind but otherwise he was blameless.

Tommy signed his statement. His daughter confirmed that she and her husband had been with him as he had stated. There were handshakes all round and that was the end of the matter. The statement would go on the case file and would, in all probability, not be referred to again.

Harry and Bob made their way back to the station where the next item on the agenda would be lunch in the staff canteen. While the morning had not been wasted in the sense that nothing they had done had taken the case forward, the fact is that a lot of police work is routine. The need to take a statement from Tommy Patterson had been just that. They had no expectation from his brief account of his dealings with Mary over the matter of arranging flowers for his unfortunate wife's funeral, and in that they were not disappointed. It was a case of filing the statement to place a small piece in the overall jigsaw of the investigation. If nothing else, it would underline the fact that they had been thorough in their enquiries and left nothing to chance.

They were now required to return to the Incident Room to resume the investigation proper. No sooner had they taken their seats and pulled out the case file than there was a knock on the Incident Room door, followed by the appearance of the eager figure of PC Doyle. The young constable had been on duty in the Grainger Market that morning, manning the temporary Incident Room in Alley 3.

For the most he was keeping a weather eye on the scene of the crime as Pauline Conlon bustled about, having been granted permission to re-open the shop and begin trading again following the horrendous events of Tuesday night and Wednesday morning.

He had found time dragging as he fulfilled his tedious task. The boss had told him he might receive visits from stall and unit holders who had remembered something relevant, but there had been nothing of interest. It was obvious that the decision to close down the temporary Incident Room at the end of today was the right one. Henceforth, the investigation was to be conducted exclusively from Market Street.

However, just as he had given up hope of any developments and was preparing to take his lunch break, he did receive a caller. As a result of what the visitor had to say, he took it upon himself to lock up the unit, return the keys to the Market Superintendent and make his way back to base post haste.

Bob Frame glanced in Doyle's direction as he made his way across the room to where he and Harry Maguire were sitting;

'Good afternoon, Doyle; what brings you back? What's the crack? Is everything quiet down at the Grainger Market, then?'

'Yes, Mr. Frame. At least it was until late this morning, but then there was a development which I thought could be important, so I came straight back here to report it.'

Doyle was quite animated and almost gabbled his words. Bob straightened his back and focussed on the young PC, intrigued;

'Go ahead then, Constable. What is it that's got you so agitated and brought you galloping back here?'

'Well sir, as I say, it had been a boring morning and not a soul had called in to see me. I was just about to give up and come back here when a young lad of about fifteen knocked on the door. My first reaction was that it was just a curiosity seeker. However, he told me he was apprenticed to Raymond Hoult, the cobbler, and he had remembered something from the night of the crime which he thought might be important.'

'Did he, by Jove? What did he have to say for himself, then?'

'Well, Mr. Frame, I thought it best to sit him down. I gave him a pencil and a couple of sheets of headed note paper. I told him to take his time and write down exactly what he had remembered, making sure he left nothing out. When he had finished, I made him read it through carefully twice. He made a couple of small changes, then said he was satisfied with it. I also asked him two supplementary questions and I have written them down as well and he added his answers.

'I signed the finished statement and put the date on it so that it was officially witnessed. I thanked him and I took his address. I know he is usually in Mr Hoult's shop but if it really is important, I thought we might need to talk to him out of hours.'

'Well done, son. Excellent work. What have you done with the statement then?' A flustered PC Doyle fished in the breast pocket of his uniform and withdrew a couple of crumpled sheets of paper which he handed over to Bob Frame. He, in turn, passed them to Harry Maguire who unfolded them without a word, smoothed them on his desk-top and began to read aloud;

STATEMENT OF THOMAS GRAHAM

My name is Thomas Graham. I am an apprentice shoemaker employed by Mr Raymond Hoult of Unit 104 in the Grainger Market. He came to see you yesterday about having worked late on Tuesday night. At that time, we were repairing a pair of gentlemen's calf leather shoes. We locked up and left the shop around about a quarter to six. Mr Hoult walks slowly on account of his gammy hip and I ran off in front of him as I was hungry and wanted to get home for my tea. I have returned to the Incident Room because I have remembered something.

As I was running towards one of the market exits, I saw somebody I recognised. It was the smell of his cigar smoke that attracted my attention in the first place, actually. You see, Mr Hoult sometimes sends me to put a bet on for him. Just small amounts; a tanner each as a rule and he is quite lucky, as a matter of fact. Anyway, the person I recognised was Davy Conlon, the bookie. I looked back over my shoulder to where the smell was coming from and he was just wandering past his wife's shop. He did not seem to be doing anything in particular, just walking along, but I thought it might be important.

In reply to a supplementary question by PC Kevin Doyle who asked if he was sure it was Mr Conlon he saw, Tommy said he was 'absolutely certain,' adding that he was carrying a Gladstone bag which he had seen him with before. He also stated that the smell of the cigar was distinctive. His actual words were 'those cigars of his stink.' Asked if he could be any more precise about the time of this encounter,

Tommy was only able to confirm that 'it was round about a quarter to six, just as I was leaving the market.' He could not be more precise than that as he does not own a watch and he never had cause to look at the market clock. He maintained the market seemed to be empty apart from Mr, Conlon, but as he was in a rush, the boy couldn't be certain. PC Doyle thanked the young man and assured him his statement would be passed on to his superiors at the earliest opportunity.

Statement verified and witnessed by PC Kevin Doyle.

Harry Maguire placed the paper on which the boy's statement was written slowly and deliberately on the desk in front of him. He sat back in his chair and exhaled slowly before looking across at PC Doyle and saying in a hushed, almost reverential tone in keeping with the significance of the statement;

'Thank you very much, Constable. This is an exemplary piece of policing and it does you a lot of credit. You did exactly the right thing and we will be following this up as a matter of urgency. Now, take yourself off to the canteen and have yourself a cup of tea. Good lad.'

A blushing and flustered Doyle? stammered his thanks and, almost tripping himself in the process in his haste, he left the room, wiped his forehead with his handkerchief and followed the boss's instructions.

To say the two detectives were pleased with Tommy Graham's statement was an understatement of the first degree. They were ecstatic. Despite all the hard work they had done in the recent days since the murder and although they had a file full of potentially valuable possibilities, this was the closest they had come to what could be a genuine breakthrough in the case.

'Bob, this could be dynamite!'

Bob Frame was, in keeping with his nature, less extravagant in his reaction, but he, too, was well aware that the sheets of paper on his guvnor's desk could prove to be a turning point in the investigation. Both men were keen to bring momentum to the situation.

'We need to get hold of Conlon and bring him in straight away' said Harry. 'He has obviously told us a pack of lies so we need to get the truth out of him.'

They made arrangements to have Davy Conlon brought in for questioning immediately, only to be extremely frustrated when they were informed that Conlon had let it be known to his wife and anyone else who cared to listen, that he and a bunch of his cronies had arranged to travel to a race meeting in York that day. They did not expect to be home until late in the evening as they had booked an evening meal at a local restaurant and aimed to catch the last train. Disappointed but philosophical, Harry and Bob advised Pauline Conlon that her husband would be required to attend Market Street police station at ten o'clock the next morning to answer some further questions in connection with the case. Anxious though they were to hear what he had to say for himself in the light of this new evidence, Davy Conlon would have to wait.

CHAPTER SEVEN

FRIDAY, 5TH OCTOBER

DETECTIVE CONSTABLE Bob Frame and Detective Sergeant Harry Maguire began their working day by briefing Detective Chief Superintendent Walton on their intentions as had become their daily practice since they had been placed in charge of the investigation into the murder of Mary Bartlett.

The news of the previous day's statement by young Tommy Graham and its potential repercussions for the case was mana from Heaven for the Chief Super, who had a considerable vested interest in a quick and successful outcome to the case.

Walton was anxious to know how the two detectives intended to approach the Conlon interview, which promised to be crucial.

'Well sir, he needs to be made aware of the trouble he is in. I am hoping that like all bullies – and he is certainly a bully – he will show his true colours when he is confronted. I don't intend to brow beat him, but he will be left in no doubt about the precarious position he is in.'

'That sounds good to me,' the Spectre replied. 'Let me know how it goes.'

The stage having been set and seemingly approved, Harry and Bob were primed and ready when Davy Conlon was ushered into the room by PC Lloyd at precisely one minute past ten. He was his usual dapper, self-absorbed and composed self. He casually removed his overcoat and handed it to the Constable to hang up, to reveal a beautifully bespoke navy blue serge suit, over a crisp white silk shirt and a plain maroon silk tie. His black leather shoes were highly polished. He was immaculate and he appeared to be completely at ease. His pompous self-confidence was reflected in the fact that he had arrived without the accompaniment of his legal representative. It was apparent he had no knowledge of young Graham's statement and was prepared for a routine interview.

Harry Maguire picked up on Conlon's demeanour immediately. He hoped to establish an early and telling advantage so, indicating to Conlon that he should take the chair opposite him, the Detective Sergeant came straight to the point;

'Mr. Conlon. Thank you for coming in. The fact is there are some aspects of your original statement which we need to go over with you again. It is my duty to advise you for the record that you are not under arrest and to confirm that you are here of your own free will. You came in response to our request and you are therefore free to leave at any time. You also have the right to ask for the presence of your solicitor. You are not a suspect at present but are nevertheless here to assist us with our enquiries. That completes the formalities and I have to ask if you are happy to co-operate and that you will answer our questions to the best of your ability.'

'Yes, of course, Sergeant Maguire. Anything I can do to help.'

Conlon's reply verged on the patronising as he smiled obsequiously, and he casually brushed the right thigh of his trouser with the palm of his hand. He presented a relaxed figure as he gazed across the desk in Harry's direction;

'Very well. Let's come straight to the point, shall we? You told us when we took your original statement, Mr. Conlon, that on the night of the murder of Mary Bartlett you did not at any time visit the interior of the Grainger Market. You also claimed that as a consequence, you specifically were never in the vicinity of your wife's flower shop.

'Your account of your movements was that you had tea at Carrick's Café on Grey Street. You then walked to Bourgogne's on Newgate Street where you had a drink before continuing to the taxi rank adjacent to Grey's monument. There you met your friend Israel Simpson, and together you took a cab to Maple Terrace, off Elswick Road, where you attended the monthly meeting of the masonic lodge of which you and Simpson are both members.

'Do you still maintain that as an accurate summary of your movements during the course of the afternoon and early evening of Tuesday, 2nd October and do you stand by that statement?'

'Yes, I do.'

'In that case, Mr. Conlon, I am obliged to inform you that I have received a statement from someone who claims to have seen you within the confines of the Grainger Market at about ten to six on Tuesday night. Is that possible?'

Conlon was clearly taken aback by the allegation, but for

the moment at least he was sticking to his story;

'No, absolutely not,' he blustered.

Harry hit back;

'The person who made this statement does know you quite well, Mr. Conlon. Indeed, it would be fair to say that you are a very well-known and recognisable figure in these parts. This individual described you very accurately, detailing the distinctive clothes you were wearing. They also made mention of the fact you were carrying a Gladstone bag in which you were no doubt carrying your items of masonic regalia. He or she also further described you as smoking a large cigar with a very distinctive smell. This witness is convinced beyond doubt it was you who was walking through the Grainger Market in the direction of the Nelson Street exit. What do you have to say to that?'

The level of detail and the purposeful manner in which Harry Maguire had presented this litany of events to him had a major effect on Conlon's mood. He had changed instantly from the over-confident and patronising individual who had sat down at the start of the interview just a few minutes earlier. There was now a wariness about him, and his expression was grim. His body language was much less positive. He gave every impression of a dawning realisation that the initiative had shifted, and he could be in real trouble. However, for the moment at least, he was not prepared to concede any ground. The pleasantries, though, were over;

'You can say what you like, Maguire, but you and I both know that what you have is purely circumstantial. It is one person's word against another's at the end of the day. You still have no convincing proof that I was anywhere near there at the time. It could simply have been someone making mischief for all you know. It wouldn't have a chance of standing up in court.'

Harry knew there was something in what Conlon said, but he remained confident that he had his adversary on the defensive, and he pressed on;

'Well, to be honest, Mr. Conlon, I am past the point where I am trying to prove where you were at the time. I am satisfied on that front. It is clear to me that you were lying in your original statement. What I now want to hear from you is why you were in the Grainger Market and why you continue to deny it. It is clear you have something to hide. My advice to you is that it would serve your best interests to change your statement and tell us the truth, so that we can eliminate you from our enquiries.'

Conlon paused for reflection. He could see a small glimmer of hope in Maguire's words. He studied the fingernails of his left hand as he gathered his thoughts and considered his next move. His dilemma was that he did not know precisely how cast iron the detective's information was. He was tempted briefly to stick to his story and brazen it out; to call Maguire's bluff in other words. On reflection, though, he knew that having dug a hole for himself with his first inaccurate statement, he needed to provide a more credible alibi to get the police off his back.

'All right,' was his ultimate response, 'it is perfectly innocent anyway. I thought I would be able to protect someone else, but my good intentions appear to have got me into trouble. As you may know, I am partial to the ladies. My wife, Pauline, knows all about my occasional indulgences and tolerates them within reason.

'I own a flat on Leazes Park Road which I keep for entertainment purposes, should we say. Unfortunately, on this occasion, which is to say Tuesday afternoon, the lady who was my companion was not only married, but also a well-known figure in the town herself. I therefore needed to be discreet. If the time we spent together became public knowledge, it could become very awkward for both of us, as you can imagine. Consequently, I had no choice but to suggest in my statement that I was elsewhere. It was in no way an attempt to mislead you about my whereabouts, just a white lie to protect the lady's reputation.

'Hence the tale I spun about having afternoon tea in Carrick's then going for a drink at Bourgogne's. The truth is that I left my flat on Leazes Park Road after putting the lady in a taxicab, then I made my way across town. By the time I got to the Grainger Market I had about an hour to spare.

'I did go for a drink, but not to Bourgogne's as I said in my statement. I went to the Café Royal on Nelson Street. I got there just before half past five. There were plenty of people in there who know me and could vouch for me.'

Harry knew he had Conlon on the run, and he was determined exploit his advantage; it was time to apply more pressure;

'You do realise you are now admitting to having been in the vicinity of the murder scene at around the time Mary Bartlett was killed? Add to that you have now conceded that you lied about your whereabouts in your previous statement. You can surely see that your defence is very precarious and lacks credibility. Unfortunately for you I am now in a position, in the light of what you have told me, where I have to regard you as a suspect.'

Conlon was now floundering. He had taken on the wild-eyed look of someone manifesting fear. He resorted to the kind of last-ditch protestations his interrogator expected from someone in his increasingly vulnerable position.

'I know it doesn't look great, Sergeant,' he pleaded, 'and I have been a fool. I know that now. I admit I am no angel, but I swear to you I am not a murderer. Why would I want to kill a young woman I barely knew? It makes no sense.'

These were the words of a man in panic, delivered more in hope than expectation. Not only that, but Davy Conlon's position was about to get worse. DC Bob Frame had assumed his familiar role in events so far. While his boss pursued his relentless grinding down of the suspect, Bob had been sitting unobtrusively in the corner of the room keeping his own counsel and constraint. He was outside of Conlon's line of vision and it is possible the suspect had forgotten about Frame's presence in the room. Bob was not a loquacious man at the best of times, but he had a well-deserved reputation for finding a telling question at the right moment in an investigation. He was about to demonstrate that talent again and this time his question was obvious and simple;

'Mr. Conlon,' he said with quiet authority, 'why did you go to your wife's shop?'

'Conlon turned quickly to look in Bob Frame's direction. He was completely taken aback by the intervention. The question had come from another person and a different direction and its surprise element had a devastating effect on his nerves and composure. He seemed to shrink in his seat like a deflated balloon. He was a man who was diminished and close to being defeated. The question had come out of the blue and he had no prepared answer.

Harry had not anticipated Bob's timely intervention, but he was instantly aware of its effect on the suspect. He knew this was a pivotal moment. These Bob Frame insights were not frequent, but they were usually timely and perceptive. Harry was not about to let the opportunity pass him by;

'Answer the man, Conlon,' he said, almost in a whisper, but with an undertone of uncharacteristic menace. He gave his adversary no time to recover his equilibrium as he drove home his advantage by repeating the question.

'Why did you go to the shop?'

Conlon was utterly undone. He realised he must now place his faith in some saving sense, born of the gravity of the situation in which he found himself, which seemed to be telling him that the only way forward was to admit the hopelessness of his situation and tell the unvarnished truth. It was the only card he had left to play. Head bowed and tone muted, he confessed;

'I knew the girl was there and I wanted to see if there was anything I could get out of her.'

There was no defiance in his words. He was a beaten man and he knew it. He spoke with shame and chagrin and such was the depth of his despair he was unable to articulate what he was trying to say. Harry Maguire was having none of it:

'Tell me exactly what you mean by that.'

'She was young and pretty and I thought I might have some success with her,' Conlon muttered almost to himself.

'You arrogant, self-serving, debauched specimen of manhood,' Harry stormed. For one of the few times in his life he was genuinely filled with fury, loathing and disgust. Conlon's words had been spoken in a murmur of fear and trepidation, but Harry responded with the emotions of a decent man. It was probably just as well he caught Bob Frame's cautionary glance from across the room in the corner of his eye. Bob's fingers were moving unobtrusively from one to ten, warning Harry to take a breath and a few seconds to calm himself before he continued. Eventually, he felt sufficiently in control of himself to continue his cross examination of the abject figure in front of him;

'I presume your advances met with no success,' he said in as neutral a tone as he could muster. He knew the answer before Conlon replied;

'That is totally correct,' was the inevitable response. 'As a matter of fact, she went bloody light. She threatened to tell Pauline and that boyfriend of hers, the Veitch kid. Apparently, he carries a butcher's knife.'

Conlon was now close to resembling a pitiful figure and his mention of Danny Veitch and the possibility of him carrying a dangerous weapon brought a shudder to his whole body. He was at the lowest of ebbs of his own devising.

To be fair, Harry Maguire was not exactly revelling in the situation. His contempt for Conlon was all-pervading, but he was deriving professional satisfaction from the way things were panning out. This was real and significant progress and he was determined to put his considerable distaste on one side and use the huge advantage he now held to see the thing through;

'Go on. Tell me what happened next.'

'She grabbed her coat and dashed past me into the market. I had my set of shop keys on my key ring, so I locked the shop and slipped off in the opposite direction. That was the last I saw of her, I swear it. I walked straight through Nelson Street exit and into the Cafe Royal where I bought a quick whisky to steady my nerves. Then I made my way to the taxi rank, as arranged, to meet Israel Simpson. That's the truth, Sergeant, on my word of honour.'

Harry snorted derisively. The word honour was absurdly incongruous coming from Conlon's lips.

'It may or may not be the truth, Conlon, but what I do know for certain is that you do not have an honourable bone in your body. There is nothing whatsoever in your story for you to be proud of. You are a shameful human being. You do realise, I assume, that poor Mary Bartlett's dead body was back in your wife's shop less than half an hour later and she was stone cold dead. I am having difficulty in working out how that could happen in such a short space of time without you being involved. You are in major trouble mate, believe me. Major trouble.

'On the basis of what you have told me, I could very well arrest you on suspicion of the murder of Mary Bartlett. I am now going to caution you, which makes you an official suspect. You do not have to say anything, but what you do say may be given in evidence. You will be released on police bail pending further enquiries. My advice to you is to contact your solicitor at the earliest opportunity. Keep yourself close and available. We will be back in touch with you, of that you can be certain. Now, get out of my sight.

You disgust me.'

Conlon made no reply. He was a completely spent force. His expression was a combination of fear and trepidation. He was escorted from the room by the duty constable and left the premises. The interview had not only reduced Davy Conlon to a state of exhaustion; Harry Maguire was also drained by the experience. He was still a young and inexperienced officer, and this was the first major case of which he had charge. He was not yet hardened to harsh reality. The story of Davy Conlon's despicable treachery and attempted debauchery had impacted seriously on Harry's sense of decency and he would need time to recover.

Having said that, there was elation as well as fatigue in his bearing as he and Bob Frame left the room. They embraced in the satisfaction of a task extremely well accomplished. He smiled wanly at his friend and fellow officer and said;

'Where did you find that one, you Scottish wizard?'

'There was no magic this time, Harry,' Bob replied, 'it was the obvious question. There could have been no other reason for him to be hanging about. He had time on his hands and Pauline would probably have told him that Mary was working late on those Patterson wreaths. By his own admission he had indulged in a few drinks and he must have acted on impulse. Being the kind of man he is, it was an opportunity he could not resist. He did not have the wits or self-control to think through the possible consequences. Couldn't avoid the temptation, I suppose.'

Harry knew that Bob's reading of the situation was flawless. Conlon was the victim of his own lascivious nature and he deserved not one jot of sympathy. The temptation to rush to judgement and charge Davy Conlon with the murder of Mary Bartlett there and then was something to be resisted, however. This was a time for calm heads. They had enough evidence to regard Conlon as a possible, even a probable killer, but they could not yet be certain. They needed to consider his new version of events in a dispassionate and detached way. Harry's first instinct was to ask for the wise counsel of his trusted colleague;

'Well Bob, what do you think? Is he our man?'

'He is certainly favourite by some distance based on the evidence we have so far. There are some possible reservations we need to consider, though. For instance, he does not seem to me to be the type of person to carry a knife. I suppose there would have been scissors and possibly knives in the shop, though, and there is also the possibility that his masonic gear includes a ceremonial knife of some sort.

'I can't see that he had any real motive to kill her, either, unless he was really scared by the girl's threats to report him to his wife and Danny Veitch. It is possible he panicked and lashed out. There would almost certainly have been evidence of Mary's blood at the scene of crime, though, if it was an impulsive killing. Then there is the matter of returning the body to the shop. Conlon is fat and out of condition and I seriously doubt he could have managed it. I know I am playing devil's advocate here to a certain extent, but these are the sort of things a decent defence lawyer would pick up on to raise doubts in the minds of the jurors. We need to be 100% sure.'

'I agree with all of that,' Harry replied, 'but one thing is for sure. If he did not kill her, he had to be the last person to see her alive apart from the murderer. It's a sure bet that she fell as she ran away from him and that is how she got the bruises on her knee and forehead and lost consciousness, but that does not necessarily explain the fatal knife wound.

'There was time for someone else to carry out the stabbing, but we keep returning to the question of why? Why would someone see Mary Bartlett running away from the flower shop, whether it was to escape Conlon's clutches or to get to the dance in town to meet her friends, and stab her? Why might someone see her fall, and kill her as she was lying there? The timescale is so tight as well.

'We still have no motive if it was not Conlon's doing. There is no chance someone was collaborating with him and it's hardly likely it was a random attack for any reason we have yet been able to fathom. I suppose we have to continue considering Danny Veitch until he comes up with someone who saw him in the Three Bulls, but that is a long shot, particularly as the forensic people reckon there is no human blood on his knives.

'Let's be honest, Bob, in terms of opportunity and motive we only have a panic killing by Conlon. I am still not sure he is our man, but he is our best bet and we might be able to build a convincing case against him. It is a real possibility he was involved in some way, but I just don't see him as a murderer. We need more before we can charge him. My instinct is to let him stew over the weekend and continue our investigations to see what else we can come up with. We got a great break when the Graham lad remembered seeing Conlon; maybe we will strike lucky again. Don't forget, we have come a very long way in a short time on this case already.' They left it at that and went to report the details of Conlon's latest interrogation to Chief Superintendent Walton as he had instructed. He studied the transcript of the interview and he agreed that while Conlon had a case to answer, they needed more substantial supporting evidence before they could consider charging him; 'Well done, both of you,' he said enthusiastically,' you have made tremendous progress in the investigation so far and we have ourselves a genuine suspect. We cannot get carried away because there are still some areas of uncertainty, but there is no doubt we are now in the driving seat as far as the search for Mary Bartlett's killer is concerned.

'Now listen, lads. You have both had a long and harrowing day, albeit a rewarding one. Get yourselves off home, take your wives out for a drink and unwind. You deserve it. Enjoy your weekend. I don't see anything dramatic happening in the next couple of days. I will keep an eye on things, just in case, but you two put your feet up and recharge your batteries. I will see you first thing on Monday morning, and we will take it from there.'

It was an ebullient speech from the Spectre, who was beginning to visualise the kudos which would come his way if his gamble in putting Maguire and Frame in charge of a major murder investigation paid dividends. He had a lot to gain, but he could pay a heavy price if they failed. In fairness, he was delighted, for their sakes as well as his own, that they appeared to be moving towards the solution of the case. They were doing a fine job, but he knew the matter was not closed. The portents were good but there was still a great deal of work to be done.

As far as Harry and Bob were concerned, they did indeed go straight home to tea with their respective families. They each reflected in their own ways on what Bob dubbed 'Conlon Day' and each of them was satisfied with where they were with the case. Neither of them was completely sure of Conlon's guilt yet, but they both knew the momentum was with them.

As it happened, neither of them took the Chief Superintendent's advice to take their wives out. That could wait until tomorrow night. Instead they both settled for an hour in front of the fire, a bottle of beer and an early night. The case was moving in a satisfactory direction and the Chief Superintendent's suggestion that they should step back, take a breath and return after the weekend afreshed, made good sense.

CHAPTER EIGHT

SATURDAY NIGHT, 6TH OCTOBER

HARRY AND Bob both slept like the proverbial logs after their mental stresses of the previous day. They even enjoyed the luxury of a lay in on Saturday morning thanks to their wives managing to keep the children more or less quiet until about nine o'clock. A hearty breakfast apiece and they were fresh and ready to face the new day.

As it was Saturday, the lads would have preferred to walk out of the top of the street, cross the road and spend the afternoon watching Newcastle United in action. Unfortunately, their plan was thwarted by the fact the Newcastle were playing away from home that day and the prospect of watching the Reserves in Central League action in front of a sparse crowd on a fresh October afternoon did not hold the same appeal. The Central League was in its first season, but it was second best by far when compared with the real thing.

Fortunately, there was another professional spectator sport just as close to hand in the shape of the New St. James' Hall boxing stadium which was, like the football ground, located just outside the top of Bulmer Street. It was actually the first building on the right and immediately adjacent. It was nothing if not convenient.

The original St. James' Hall had been erected on the same site in 1909. It had a capacity of 3,000 spectators and it had proved to be so popular that another, larger stadium was built to house 4,000 people. The 'New' St. James' Hall was opened in 1930, just four years previously, and it was a splendid, custom built indoor arena. The opening night saw a full house in attendance with local favourite Jack Casey, the man they called the 'Sunderland Assassin,' topping the bill. Like its predecessor, New St. James' Hall quickly became a popular venue and bills, often featuring a good sprinkling of local talent, were held on most Saturday nights.

Bob and Harry could best be described as occasional visitors. Although they were not necessarily fanatical boxing fans, they found the entertainment relaxing at the end of a demanding week's work. Plus, they admired the skill and bravery of the participants.

In the absence of any compelling afternoon entertainment across the road at St. James' Park they chose to go to the boxing this Saturday evening. They were attracted by the fact that the bill comprised contests which were exclusively between local prospects who could be relied upon to put on a decent show in front of a partisan crowd. The Hall was not filled to capacity, but there was a more than decent attendance and a lively atmosphere was guaranteed.

Harry and Bob had scarcely taken their seats at 6:30 when the first bout of the evening was announced over the tannoy. It turned out to be a short night of endeavour for the unfortunate Billy Wells, who hailed from Rowlands Gill in County Durham. He had the misfortune to walk on to a left hook which was delivered with considerable venom by Joe Baldesara from Sunderland in the opening round. The blow sent the hapless Wells crashing to the canvas where he lay motionless as the referee counted from one to ten, before raising Baldesara's arm in victory.

It was a dramatic start to the evening. Still, with bouts including Mick Conroy against Ray Burns, Billy Tansey versus Tommy Burns and Peter Miller up against Jim Brady, there was plenty of action still to come. Bob and Harry, however, were under strict instructions to leave the boxing hall and collect their wives by nine o'clock. They were required to meet the ladies and adjourn to the Ordnance Arms at the other end of the street for an hour of conviviality in the pub.

Meanwhile, their focus was firmly on the action. The announcer was introducing the protagonists for the second contest of the evening when Bob Frame tapped Harry on the arm and pointed discreetly in the direction of the upper-level seats where two young men were hunched together in earnest conversation;

'What do you make of that, Harry. Is that a sight for sore eyes or what?'

Harry was surprised to realise that the two individuals Bob had drawn to his attention were Danny Veitch and Gordon Hugill;

'I didn't know those two were mates. It would be very interesting to know what the pair of them are talking about. They look positively conspiratorial.'

Bob paused, torn between the action and Harry's interest

in Veitch and Hugill, before replying;

'Maybe they are just fight fans. In any case, it could be time for us to have a little chat with young Mr Hugill and find out. What do you think? Bring him in for questioning on Monday morning?'

Harry nodded in agreement and the two men returned their attention to the boxing. When one of the contestants in a later bout flattened his unsuspecting opponent in the third round on the stroke of a quarter to nine, Bob and Harry took it as their cue to leave. It had been a lively night in the ring and the sight of Veitch and Hugill in such animated conversation had been an added bonus.

The Frames and the Maguires joined their parents and in-laws in the Ordnance and enjoyed the rest of a pleasant Saturday night. The mood was relaxed and Harry was happy to respond just before 'last orders' was called, to requests to 'give us a song, Harry lad.' He had a good voice and usually obliged when the punters asked for a rendition.

He produced a polished rendition of the new Tolchard Evans composition '(If) They Made Me a King' and he even responded to light-hearted calls for more by trying out a song he had recently heard in the hit Ruby Keiller film '42nd Street,' which was currently doing the rounds, called 'You're Getting to be a Habit With Me.'

As the eight of them made their way on the short walk up Bulmer Street, Harry turned to Bob and summed up their evening;

'Canny night, Bob.'

'Aye, canny night right enough, Harry. Canny day as well'

CHAPTER NINE

MONDAY, 8TH OCTOBER

When Harry and Bob returned to duty there was a briskness in their stride and an anticipation in their minds as they took their usual way from home to work. They were not in any way deterred by the unexpected return of the gloomy and depressing early morning weather. On the contrary, they felt alert and ready to return to the case.

While Davy Conlon remained a solid suspect, they needed to firm up the evidence against him if they were to present a cast iron case. Their first priority, however, was to advise the Chief Superintendent of their observation of Danny Veitch and Gordon Hugill deep in conversation on Saturday night at the boxing hall. It was their intention to bring Hugill in for questioning on that basis. They were mindful, too, of the fact that he worked for Mickler and Goldberg and he had a working connection with Israel Simpson. He was also the boyfriend of Betty Forster and it was possible he would provide some useful background. A nod and a murmur of approval from their boss and they were on their way.

They went straight to the Incident Room and instructed

PC Lloyd to go across to the Grainger Market and bring Hugill in for questioning. PC Lloyd returned, accompanied by the young man, just before ten o'clock. He was taken straight to the Interview Room to face the two detectives. DS Maguire reminded him that they had met briefly the previous week when Hugill came to collect Betty Forster following her interview.

After formally introducing DC Frame, Harry began to speak;

'Hello Gordon. Thank you for coming in. This should not take long. As you know, the police are investigating the murder of Mary Bartlett last Tuesday. DC Frame and I are the officers in charge of the case, and we felt it would be useful to have a word with you to help fill in some of the background. We know you are Betty Forster's boyfriend. We are also aware that Betty was Mary Bartlett's best friend. These are just routine questions and you have nothing to worry about. Are you all right with that?

'Y-y-yes, Sergeant.'

Despite his speech impediment, Gordon Hugill gave the initial impression of being quite relaxed and self- possessed. Wearing his pin striped worked suit, he looked presentable, though his tie was marginally off centre as though he had dressed in haste. He looked slightly over-weight and was of just over average height. His only distinguishing features were his prominent ears and the rather unusual grey shade of his eyes. His hair was a boring brown colour and he had a pasty complexion. In summary he was an unremarkable looking 24 year old. He was from the same mould as his girlfriend, though Betty had the advantage of pretty eyes and lovely blonde hair. She had also proven to be a perceptive girl behind her timid and self-effacing manner. It would be interesting to see how Gordon compared.

Harry continued;

'I am presuming, Gordon, that you knew Mary through Betty, seeing as they were such good friends. Am I right?'

'Yes, s-s-sir. They had b-b-been b-b-best friends for ages and we all went to the d-d-dances together at the Oxford regularly, s-s-so I knew Mary p-p-pretty well.'

'Did you like her?'

'Oh yes, d-d-definitely. She was a very n-n-nice girl; very friendly and always ch-ch-cheerful. She was somebody you felt you could trust and rely on and she never had a b-b-bad word for anyone.'

'How did you feel when you found out what had happened to her, Gordon?'

'I was really sh-sh-shocked. She was not the t-t-t-type of girl you would expect the be mixed up in anything. She was d-d-decent. I c-c-could not believe it. Poor girl wouldn't hurt a f-f-fly. I was c-c-completely thunder struck when I heard she was dead. It was very upsetting to b-b-be honest.'

'Tell me about what happened on Tuesday night as far as you were concerned. You were meant to go to the dance, but I understand from Betty that you were late. How did that happen? Was there any special reason?'

'N-N-No, not really. I just stopped off at the Eldon Grill for a quick d-d-drink; it is not far from there to the Oxford. I usually pop in there for a pint on my way t t-t-to the dance. To be p-p-perfectly honest, dancing is not really my thing. I think most of the l-l-lads are the same. A quick d-d-drink helps me to relax and have the confidence to go on the dance floor. I am p-p-pretty hopeless, but it pleases Betty; she l-l-loves dancing.'

'I can sympathise with you on that,' Harry retorted with a grin, though that was not strictly true. He was really quite a passable dancer and had actually met Doris at a dance. They still went dancing from time to time. His comment was strictly in the way of keeping Gordon relaxed and forthcoming.

'Just for the record, Gordon,' Harry continued, 'is there anyone who can confirm that you were in the Eldon that night?'

Hugill looked across at Harry quizzically. It was not a question he had been expecting and, although he did not challenge it, his reply was rather resentful;

'As a m-m-matter of fact there is someone who can vouch for me. John Ryan, who is one of the b-b-barmen, is a good friend of mine. We are both Newcastle supporters and we g-g-go to the m-m-match together. We were chatting about the football and that was -p-p-part of the reason why I was a b-b-bit late.'

'That's fine. I have to ask everyone the same question as a matter of routine, as I am sure you understand,' Harry said in his most pacifying and reasonable tone, 'I suppose everyone noticed Mary had not turned up. Did it cause much comment or concern that she was missing?'

'No, not really. A few of us g-g-go regularly and there is always s-s-someone missing. We were talking among ourselves when we were not d-d-dancing and I think everybody just assumed Mary had been working l-l-later than she expected. It was not really c-c-commented on.'

'What about at the end of the night, Gordon? Did you walk Betty home?'

'Of course. I always d-d-do. We left the dance hall at about half past n-n-nine and I dropped her off at her house at around about t-t-ten to t-t-ten. Then I went straight home from there.'

'That's great. Now I would like to change the subject a little. I know from my interview with Betty that the pair of you both work for Mickler and Goldberg the jewellers. What exactly is it you do there?'

'I mend some of the d-d-damaged and broken jewellery people bring in, Most of what I do is fairly b-b-basic work like snapped chains. I will remove a damaged link and replace it with a n-n-new one. It has to be the p-p-proper shape and size. We buy a lot of spares b-b-because it is regular work. You would be amazed how c-c-careless people are with their jewellery. Also, we get pieces brought in which are not of very good quality and are easily d-d-damaged.'

Gordon was relaxed and clearly enjoyed talking about his work and Harry was content to let him do so. He was not about to reveal anything shattering about the murder, but Harry wanted to lead him on a little further, in the direction of Israel Simpson, about whom he still did not know nearly enough.

'It is pretty b-b-basic to tell you the truth, Mr. Maguire. The c-c-customers usually wait while I carry out their r-r-repairs. If the work is any more complicated or it needs any t-t-tricky adjustments, Mr. Mickler will tell the customer they will have to leave it for a d-d-day or two for the repair to be carried out. Mr. Simpson d-d-does all the repairs which I can't do because I have not been trained on them yet. He is b-b-brilliant. He can mend anything!'

This was more like it. The interview was now in the territory Harry had been hoping for. Gordon's stutter was diminishing as he talked about his work and he was on familiar ground. His willingness to talk about Israel Simpson presented Harry with the opportunity to learn more about the enigmatic jeweller. Any further light which Gordon could shed could only be useful.

'Do you see a lot of Mr. Simpson then, Gordon?'

'Very much s-s-so,' the young man replied guilelessly, 'It is a bit of a strange arrangement really. I work for Mr. Mickler and Mr. Goldberg, but I spend quite a lot of my t-t-t-time with Mr. Simpson in his shop on the other side of the m-m-market. I suppose we are b-b-both employed by Mickler and Goldberg, but Mr. Simpson runs his own business as well. That is where he has his workshop. I suppose you c-c-could say I am his apprentice.

'He t-t-taught me how to do the small repairs I carry out so far. He always keeps a c-c-close eye on me and he is beginning to teach me other bits and pieces all the time. He trusts me to do the things he has t-t-taught me b-b-b-but the finished repair still has to pass his scrutiny before the item c-c-can be returned to the customer especially if it is a new skill I have been t-t-taught.

'Mr. Simpson sets high standards. He is an excellent t-t-t-teacher. At the moment he is showing me how to adjust the f-f-fit of a ring. I sometimes reduce them by putting them in the vice by heating them. The ring is then d-d-dropped into a smaller mould and allowed the cool. I also know how t-t-t-to expand them if the customer says the ring is too t-t-tight. We have a special tool for that, b-b-but the work still involves heating the ring to make it pliable.

'As I said, Mr. Simpson is very clever. I am hoping that eventually I will b-b-be able to work as a properly qualified jewellery repairer. C-c-come to think of it, that is probably why Mr. Goldberg and Mr. Mickler encourage Mr. Simpson to teach me, so that I will be able to t-t-take over from him some day.'

This was going better than Harry could have imagined. Just like Betty Forster, Gordon was opening up without any inhibitions and his answers were providing some very useful background to the character of Israel Simpson. He decided to press on;

'What else does Mr. Simpson show you or explain to you, Gordon? Does he give you any advice?'

'Well, he always says I need to know something completely before I can move on. I need to be able to do things without asking for help before he will show me something new. He has this saying about patience being a virtue and I must be prepared to take my time.

'He has begun explaining to me a little about the different kinds and colours of precious stones that go into rings. It is very complicated and hard to remember. I make notes and take them home to learn, which Mr. Simpson seems to think is a good idea. He is right when he says you can't rush things, whether it is how to do repairs or to learn about the stones. Mr. Simpson does not always have the time to go over things too often. He has his own work to do and it is sometimes very complicated.

'I think he understands how k-k-keen I am to learn and improve and I appreciate that I am just a b-b-b-beginner, but I want to become what he calls accomplished. When I first started I was a b-b-bit lazy if I am being honest, b-b-but that was because I thought the job was boring. Since I started learning from Mr. Simpson it is m-m-much more interesting and I look forward to going to work every morning. If I can keep working and learning from Mr. Simpson, I could have a g-g-good career.'

Harry felt it was time to move on. Hugill had told him as much as he was likely to as far as Simpson was concerned.

'Okay, Gordon. This is all very interesting background detail for us, but I want to move on. We won't keep you much longer. Let me ask you about Saturday night.'

A puzzled look came over Hugill's face. He had been quite happy to talk about his work, though he could not understand what it had to do with Mary Bartlett's murder. This was different, and he was more uneasy and apprehensive if the police wanted to talk about his social life.

'Detective Constable Frame and I were at the boxing at St. James' Hall and we happened to see you and Mary's boyfriend, Danny Veitch there. Are you boxing fans?'

This was a definite departure. The question took young Hugill by surprise. He was not sure where the interview was going and he was momentarily lost for an answer. His eyes darted warily between the two policemen. He gulped and began talking again;

'D-D-Danny l-l-likes the boxing m-m-more than m-m-me, b-b-but we sometimes m-m-meet up at S-S-St.

J-J-James' Hall. We d-d-don't always s-s-stay for the whole n-n-night. We m-m-might n-n-nip off for a quick p-p-pint b-b-before we g-g-go home.'

Harry and Bob could not help but notice the deterioration in Hugill's speech pattern. His stammering was much more pronounced, which they took as an indication that he was nervous and apprehensive. It would be interesting to find out why.

'So, are you and Danny big mates then?'

Again, the lad hesitated. His expression had taken on a more furtive and defensive appearance and he was about to choose his words with greater care;

'I w-w-would n-n-not say b-b-big mates exactly. I knew D-D-Danny b-b-before, but we have been in other's c-c-company m-m-more lately. That has b-b-been b-b-because of the girls. I s-s-suppose you could say we g-g-get on w-w-well enough.'

Harry knew he had to be careful where he took this conversation. Hugill was on edge and tentative and he might well clam up if Harry pushed too hard. On the other hand, there was something discordant about the way the conversation was going and Harry was anxious to unearth the reason why if he possibly could.

'Were you talking about anything in particular the other night, then?'

'No. n-n-not really. We were just t-t-talking about the b-b-boxing and about w-w-work. Just routine s-s-stuff. Nothing s-s-special.'

Harry was convinced Hugill was hiding something. His whole demeanour had changed since the name of Danny

Veitch had come up in the conversation. He was either afraid of Danny for some reason, or they were up to something together. Hugill's unease was manifest and his account of his chat with Veitch was superficial. Harry wanted to press harder, but he knew it would serve no useful purpose. Hugill was clearly reluctant to say much more and it might be best to leave things there and keep their powder dry for another day.

'Well, Gordon. Thank you for your time. What you have told us has been very useful. We will call it a day for now, shall we? If we should need to speak to you again, we know where we can find you. For the present, though, you are free to go.'

Gordon Hugill left the police station in a perplexed frame of mind. He could not be regarded as a highly intelligent individual, but he did have a measure of shrewdness. He knew the police officer who had interviewed him was probing for something. He just could not fathom out what it was. Still, the ordeal was over now and he decided his best plan was to put it from his mind and carry on as normal.

Harry, meanwhile, looked across at his colleague with raised eyebrows to get his reaction. The Scotsman had followed the interview with close interest. He knew Harry would be asking him to comment and he was ready;

'That was very interesting, Guv. More so than I had expected. He was perfectly relaxed and quite outgoing early on when he was talking about his work at the jewellers. His observations about Israel Simpson provided us with some useful additions to his profile but they were not exactly world shattering.

'He does not seem to be more than a basic apprentice who has a lot to learn, but Simpson appears to have taken a shine to him and lit a spark under him. He is obviously motivated in a way he was not before Simpson began to encourage him. He said himself he was more ambitious now where previously he had been an idle so-and-so.

'It was when you asked him about his friendship with Danny Veitch that he seemed to undergo a personality change, He was much more guarded, and twitchy, and his stammer got worse as if he was feeling tense and under pressure.'

Bob's summary was spot on as usual. Harry nodded;

'He was certainly keen to play down his relationship with Danny Veitch. It is obvious that they are mates. They were at the boxing together and they went for a pint afterwards; that is what mates do, but he was distinctly sheepish about their friendship. What do you think? Are they up to something? If so, what might it be?'

'It's hard to tell. I agree they could be in cahoots, though. Maybe they do a spot of petty pilfering they don't want us to know about, but I do not see either of them as a hardened criminal. I am still to be convinced that Danny Veitch is as bad as people like to paint him. As far as Hugill goes, I suspect he is a follower rather than a leader. By his own admission he was a lazy article without ambition not so long ago and you know what they say about leopards and their spots.

'Maybe he sees Danny Veitch in a similar light to Simpson. Veitch is a strong character and Hugill may have fallen under his spell. I suspect he does not have many mates and he is glad to hang around with Danny Veitch and do his bidding. He seems to me to be a bit of a softy. After all, if a quiet, naïve girl like Betty Forster can keep him under her wing, he is not likely to be rampaging around the place stabbing young women with a butcher's knife.

'We only wanted two things from him; to find out how close he was to Veitch and we still have work to do on that. Then to get some of the inside track on Israel Simpson. What he gave us was interesting, but it did not really light any bright illuminations.

'Let's keep an eye on him and see if there is anything else to be learned. It will be interesting if he does turn up in Veitch's company again in the next day or two. I don't think we can link him to the murder in any direct way. He isn't a suspect. He is more of a fringe player, really. He isn't of interest apart from his links to Simpson and Betty Forster and the fact that he works at Mickler and Goldberg's.'

Bob only had one more point to make before they moved on from Gordon Hugill;

'I think the link with Simpson is worth watching. Simpson feels sorry for him, but is he helping him out of the goodness of his heart, do you think, or does he have an ulterior motive?'

'I have no idea Bob. The kid obviously thinks the world of him, but I do not see it as useful. Unfortunately, we learned nothing to take the spotlight away from Davy Conlon.'

That seemed to be that. Bob and Harry were usually in accord and if Bob Frame felt he could offer a different perspective Harry always encouraged him to do so. In this case, Bob had a strong feeling that Harry's analysis was close to the mark and he was inclined to go along with it. However, there was something about Gordon Hugill which gave him cause for unease. He had not been able to put his finger on it yet and it would niggle away inside him until he could. He would keep it to himself for the present, but what he did know was that when he had felt this way in the past, he had invariably been right.

CHAPTER TEN

TUESDAY, 9TH OCTOBER

THE MORNING of Mary Bartlett's funeral brought with it a hazy sunshine which gave promise of a brightness to come. Funerals are dour and sad occasions at the best of times, but a sunny day at least goes some way to lifting the depressed spirits of the mourners who gather for the occasion.

Mary was to be buried at St. Andrew's cemetery. She had been a regular member of the congregation in the parish church on Newgate Street and it was fitting that she should be laid to rest in the church's burial ground. The cemetery was located just off the Great North Road as it made its way out of the city centre on its way towards the border with Scotland seventy miles away.

St. Andrew's cemetery came into existence when its first internment took place in 1857. It was known originally as St. Andrew's and Jesmond cemetery as it was located in the well-to-do suburb of Jesmond, but it reverted to plain St. Andrew's cemetery four years later. Among items of special interest was the fact that there were 138 victims of the Great War buried in St. Andrew's. About thirty of them were laid to rest in a dedicated war graves plot.

Harry and Bob had both decided to attend Mary's funeral. They did so out of respect for the victim and her family, but they were also present in their professional capacity as the two detectives in charge of the search for Mary's murderer. They would be making a careful note of those members of the congregation who had any connection with their investigations, as well as looking out for anything which might be unusual or of interest.

They were not expecting anything dramatic to take place, but it would be remiss to ignore the general comings and goings. Both men had been touched and horrified by the dreadful fate which had befallen this innocent and very well thought of young woman.

The murder had attracted a great deal of publicity through the local newspapers. There was widespread outrage at the apparently senseless act, and this accounted in some measure for the large turn out of mourners. These included Bob and Harry's boss, Chief Superintendent Ken Walton who was representing the city police. He cut a striking figure in the full uniform of his rank; a fact of which he was very much aware and in which he took both pride and satisfaction.

The Chief Superintendent travelled separately from his two officers and was there purely as a respectful mourner, Harry and Bob on the other hand made their way together, arriving on foot at just after a quarter to eleven. As it had promised earlier, the sun came out just as the two detectives arrived at the cemetery and the scene was set, thankfully, for a bright send-off to bring down the curtain, as it were, on a young life which had promised so much but was ended in a tragic and devastating fashion.

Harry and Bob made a point of mingling with the other mourners as they waited outside the chapel for the arrival of the hearse. The majority were unknown to them. Neither of them had any previous dealings with the Bartlett family and spotted only a handful of people they recognised. They chatted briefly with Mr. and Mrs. Forster, the parents of Mary's best friend. Betty, for her part, was arm-in-arm with her boyfriend Gordon Hugill. He gave them a cautious half smile before diverting his gaze in the direction of his highly polished shoes. Betty was very subdued and already close to tears in anticipation of the harrowing events to come.

Danny Veitch could be seen standing a few yards away, seemingly intent on keeping a low profile. On his arm was a tall, attractive and slightly over-weight girl who looked to be a couple of years his senior. The two policemen rightly assumed her to be his sister. Mary's former employer, the person who had suffered the misfortune of finding her corpse a week ago, Pauline Conlon, was a significant presence. She broke away from a small group of ladies who were friends and fellow shop and stall holders in the Grainger Market and strode purposefully in the direction of Bob and Harry.

'Hello Sergeant, Constable. I do so hate funerals, don't you?'

Without waiting for a reply, she ploughed on;

'I had to come, though, for poor Mary's sake. Judging by the number of people who have been through the shop ordering flowers I think we can expect a good turn-out, which is only right.'

Harry and Bob murmured their pleasure at seeing her and expressed the hope that she was beginning to come to terms with the tragedy. They made no mention of her errant husband, Davy Conlon, who was conspicuous by his absence. Before re-joining her friends, Mrs. Conlon was at pains to point out that she had 'pushed the boat out' in terms of the floral tributes she had provided;

'It is only right that someone like Mary, who loved flowers and spent all her working life preparing lovely floral tributes for other people, should be done proud herself. I've done me best for the lass. I hope she will be pleased.'

Mrs. Conlon, like all the other mourners, was distressed by the implications of the funeral service they would be attending in a few moments, but she seemed to be feeling it more than most, which was to be expected considering the circumstances of her role in the affair.

On the stroke of eleven o'clock the hearse carrying the body of Mary Bartlett drove slowly and majestically through the North Road cemetery gates and eventually came to a halt at the St. Andrew's chapel. As the coffin was lowered from the vehicle, Mary's immediate family made their way into the place of worship for the funeral service which was to be conducted by the Vicar of St. Andrew's. Mrs. Bartlett, Mary's widowed mother, presented a tearful but dignified figure as she was supported on either arm by her sister and brother-in-law. They took their places on the front pew and the chapel filled slowly and respectfully with the immediate family, followed by the rest of the mourners, numbering perhaps fifty in all. The pall bearers carried the coffin down the centre aisle and laid it carefully on a trestle in front of the altar.

Pauline Conlon had been as good as her word. The coffin was festooned with white lilies, while lavish bouquets were laid on the marble floor beneath. Murmurs of appreciation could be heard from the congregation as the priest slowly climbed the steps to take his place in the lectern. The Order of Service was conducted in silence, but for the obligatory prayers and appropriate readings from the scriptures. The singing of the chosen hymns, 'Abide with Me' and 'Nearer My God to Thee' was rendered with that mixture of gusto, reverence and tentative embarrassment which was typical of such occasions. The overall effect as the voices echoed around the chapel, was one of pleasant mellifluence.

The vicar delivered his moving eulogy in sonorous tones of authority and sincerity. He began by making reference to 'the tragic loss which unites us in grief and sadness here this morning.' He went on to say;

'Mary Bartlett was a young woman in the prime of her life and that life was snatched away from her in the cruellest and most savage of fashions. We can but wonder at the mind of the person who carried out this most despicable of acts. Mary was loved by all who knew her. She was kind and thoughtful in her dealings with her family, her friends and those with whom she came into contact in her work. She was a talented and conscientious florist and it is fitting that we are surrounded here by a beautiful and exuberant array. It presents a moving illustration which echoes the skills she herself possessed.

'The world is a poorer place for Mary Bartlett's departure from it and we send our deepest and warmest thoughts and prayers to her family. In particular, we extend our love and sympathy to Mary's dear mother. Already touched by tragedy with the loss of her dear late husband, her life is now torn asunder once again by this unimaginable loss of a daughter, snatched from her so cruelly.

'There is perhaps no greater tragedy than the loss of a child before her parent. There are no words of ours that can adequately describe the heartache Mrs. Bartlett must be feeling at this time. You, her family and friends, who have shared the experience of this sad occasion will, I know, continue to show love and compassion to her at this unbearable time and in the weeks to come. Let us all place our trust in Almighty God that he may look down on Mary's mother and her close family. May he bless them, keep them and bestow his love upon them. Amen.'

The priest's words had a sobering impact on everyone present and as the mourners made their way from the chapel to the actual burial site outside in the graveyard, the plaintiff sobbing of Mrs. Bartlett could be heard resonating throughout the chapel and in the near distance. There were abundant tears on all sides as people remembered the girl they had come to mourn and whose sweet nature and winning ways had touched them all in one way or another.

Mrs. Bartlett stood supported by her closest relatives as the congregation filed out of the church, some to attend the burial, others to make their way to the exit. Bob and Harry paused to offer her their sympathy;

'Mrs. Bartlett, I'm DS Maguire and this is DC Frame. We are the officers investigating Mary's death. We wish to extend our sincere condolences and promise we are doing our utmost to find the perpetrator.'

Mrs. Bartlett was a mother in mourning who had lost her only child in unimaginable circumstances, and she was clearly greatly distressed, but she replied with firmness and dignity;

'Thank you, officers. I appreciate your kind thoughts and I am sure you are doing your best. My Mary is gone and now she is being buried, but I won't be able to have peace of mind until her killer is caught. Please find him for Mary's sake as well as mine.'

It was a heartfelt plea and Mary's mother needed a handkerchief from her brother-in-law to dab away her tears. Harry squeezed her arm gently;

'Rest assured, we'll catch him or her and bring them to justice. As soon as we have anything to report we will come to see you and let you know.'

'Thank you so much, Mr. Maguire.'

Neither Harry nor Bob stayed to attend the internment in the graveyard. They regarded that as a moment for the family to come together and say their last tragic farewells to their loved one. They would be able to take some small comfort from the large number of people who had attended the funeral service as well as from the kind, measured and impassioned words of the priest in the course of his eulogy. They would remember the lovely sunny day when Mary left them for the last time, and they would talk about the magnificent floral tributes which had adorned the occasion as a reminder of her life. Nothing, though, would heal a mother's heartache as she contemplated the fact that she would have to endure the rest of her life without her beloved daughter. The healing process would be a very long and difficult one.

If Harry Maguire and Bob Frame had been determined to find the killer of Mary Bartlett, to serve justice and see him punished, they now each made a silent vow to redouble their efforts to bring this sordid and tragic case to a swift and satisfactory end for the sake of Mary's mother. It was a subdued and thoughtful pair that left the cemetery and crossed the North Road. Their intention was to walk down the side of the Town Moor.

They would cut across Exhibition Park in the direction of the Royal Victoria Infirmary and then cross over to the Trent House pub. There had been talk in the immediate aftermath of the funeral that some of the mourners would be congregating there. While neither Bob or Harry were afternoon drinkers as a rule, they had the Chief Superintendent's blessing to put in an appearance, on the basis that you never know what you might pick up from the social chat in a pub after a funeral.

The two of them had not been in any particular hurry as they strolled into town. They were still coming to terms with their emotions and needed time to gather themselves. Meanwhile, they were in a reflective mood. Their conversation was, for the most part, desultory. Harry broke the silence between them;

'Well, at least the funeral did the poor lass justice. A good turn out and, to be fair, Pauline Conlon played a blinder with the flowers. The vicar was impressive as well. Sometimes they can be tedious, or seem to be going through the motions, but he obviously sensed the mood. What he said was spot on. He really spoke with passion.'

'Yes, I suppose it is a matter of moving on now for the girl's mother and the rest of her family. Whether it's Davy Conlon or whoever it is, we owe them a swift solution. To be honest we didn't learn a great deal at the funeral, Guv. Pauline had obviously given her old man strict instructions to stay well away. Danny Veitch and Gordon Hugill were with their own people and their paths never crossed. No sign of either Simpson or Raymond Hoult, but there was no reason why either of them should be there. It would have been of more interest if Simpson had turned up.'

The Trent House pub stood on the corner of Leazes Lane, occupying numbers 1 and 2. It was a popular watering hole with a reputation for selling good ale in a convivial atmosphere. It was diagonally opposite and close to St. James' Park, hence it was always packed on match days before the kick off. The Bartlett's would be having a private get together just a couple of hundred yards away in Mary's mother's modest home on Terrace Place. Danny Veitch and his sister who lived just five doors along the street, could be expected to put in an appearance. All-in-all it was a sensible place for the mourners to gather, bearing in mind its location was near the town centre, though far enough away not to be very busy at lunch time.

Harry and Bob finally arrived after their slow walk from the cemetery and accordingly some of the fleeter of foot were already ensconced at the bar counter, glasses in hand, winding down after the morning's tribulations. As far as the lads were concerned it was to prove a fruitless trip, except in one small but possibly significant respect.

There was a potentially lively group of ladies in one corner of the lounge, the only room where women were admitted. Here the redoubtable Pauline Conlon was holding court, but otherwise the pub was quiet and the atmosphere subdued. The Forster family were presumably at Mrs. Bartlett's house where Gordon Hugill would be keeping Betty company and the number of mourners in the Trent House was small in comparison with Harry's expectations. Nevertheless, there was one person of interest who immediately claimed the attention of Harry and Bob.

It would have been a major surprise if Danny Veitch had failed to put in an appearance bearing in mind the proximity of his parents' house and, sure enough, there he was standing at the bar counter chatting to his sister. It was too good an opportunity to miss, so Harry and Bob strolled slowly across to have a word with him.

'Now then, Danny. How are tricks?' Harry ventured casually

'Mustn't grumble, Mr. Maguire,' Danny replied in similar vein, seemingly unfazed and allowing himself a small grin.

Harry would normally have left it at that, but he was encouraged by Danny's apparent lack of hostility and continued;

'This is your sister I presume,' he said, nodding in the woman's direction.

'That is right. This is wor Barbara. Barbara meet Sergeant Maguire and Constable Frame, the bobbies who are leading the hunt for Mary's murderer.'

The girl replied with a guarded smile but, like her brother, she seemed not to be disconcerted by their presence;

'Pleased to meet you.'

Danny drained his glass then turned to the police officers; 'I don't want to be rude,' he said as he fastened his coat, 'but we are only having the one. I need to get along home and put the fire on for me mam coming in and Barbara has to get back to work'

'That is not a problem, Danny. You are not going back to work then?' Harry replied, the soul of geniality.

'No, I've taken the day off. It seemed to be the sensible thing to do in the circumstances and the boss was canny about it. Anyway, I'll see you around,' he said by way of closing the conversation.

With that, Danny and Barbara Veitch made their way towards the exit. Then, just before he stepped outside, Danny hesitated and half-turned to face the detectives. He took a small step towards them, then he appeared to change his mind, turned on his heels and left the premises.

'Mmm, that was strange,' Harry Maguire mused, 'Danny seems to have something on his mind. Any ideas, Bob?'

'Not really. Possibly he is concerned about our interest in him and Gordon Hugill. Gordon is sure to have mentioned it to him after his interview. Maybe he was of a mind to ask us about it, then had second thoughts.'

Bob Frame's mind, on the other hand, was working overtime. He reminded himself of his recent instinct that there was something about Hugill that was not straightforward. He still had not fathomed out what it was but this little incident with Danny Veitch reinforced his idea that there was something he and Harry were missing about the two young men. Until he was able to form a clearer picture, he contented himself by observing;

'I am more or less convinced there is something going on there, but I have not been able to put my finger on it yet.'

Harry was content to take Bob's comment on board and await developments. Past experience told him that when Bob got his teeth into something, he would worry away at it like a dog at a bone until he came up with something. Both men knew how these little notions of Bob's often panned out. Harry was happy to let his partner keep his own counsel until he had something worthwhile to say.

CHAPTER ELEVEN

WEDNESDAY EVENING, 10TH OCTOBER

THE FRAME'S and the Maguire's were good friends and neighbours. Four of the houses in Bulmer Street were home to members of the two families and the close-knit nature of the street was reflected in their relationship. They got together socially as an eight-some each weekend for the ritual 'Saturday night out' in the Ordnance Arms at the bottom of the street. It presented a weekly opportunity for the women to brag about their bairns, while the men folk talked – and argued – about the fortunes and misfortunes of Newcastle United, the talent or lack of it on display at St. James' Boxing Hall and anything else that came up for discussion. The only topic which was forbidden was work!

The whole night was a way of unwinding; a means of forgetting for a while the pressures of work for Harry and Bob. It was also a distraction from the vagaries of bringing up small children for Doris and Ena. The grandparents joined in the chat and simultaneously took on the role of babysitters. They had a system whereby every ten minutes one of the four grandparents, armed with two house keys, would dash up the street to check whether the kids were still asleep. It was a system which suited everybody, and it worked well.

The main advantage in social terms of both couples having parents living in the street was that there were no problems involved in organising babysitters. Consequently, the young 'uns would go out from time to time, either as a couple or a foursome, in midweek if their finances and fancies made it a tempting proposition. On special occasions, such as birthdays or anniversaries, one or other couple would treat themselves to one of the more expensive and therefore better-quality entertainments on offer. Usually though, they were quite content with more basic fare.

All four were partial to live entertainment in the form of Music Hall or light-hearted plays and they had also developed a liking for the increasingly popular films of the day. They were fortunate that the centre of Newcastle close to their homes, could boast several venues where any of their preferences could be indulged.

The principal 'legitimate' theatre in town was the splendidly appointed Theatre Royal, majestically located at the top of Grey Street. The theatre had been built in 1837 as a landmark construction in Richard Grainger's 'Graingertown' vision for the city. Sadly, the original building was severely damaged by a fire during a performance of William Shakespeare's 'Macbeth.' However, it rose like the proverbial phoenix from the ashes. A major and highly praised renovation took place in 1899, based on blueprints provided by the renowned theatre designer, Frank Matcham.

The theatre was alleged to have a ghost. The story was that 'The Grey Lady of the Gallery' was a young woman who had fallen in love with one of the actors in a particular production and her love was reciprocated. The couple had planned to run away together after an evening performance. Unfortunately, the gentleman concerned had cold feet and made it clear he did not intend to proceed with the elopement. Heartbroken by his rejection, the 'Grey Lady' leaned forward from her position in the gallery on what would prove to be the last time she would see her erstwhile lover as he made his entrance. In her attempt to gain a better view of her loved one as he entered the action, she suffered the ultimate misfortune. Whether by accident or design is not recorded, but either way she fell to her death. Her apparition is said to wander the theatre to this day and there are many creditable accounts of her doing so from theatregoers who swear to have seen her.

Both in terms of price and personal preference, Harry and Bob and their wives were normally content with an evening at one of the less elitist venues in town.

Harry's pleasant singing voice and his willingness to entertain a small audience in the Ordnance Arms on a Saturday night might make him a kindred spirit of sorts. Though he would be reluctant to admit it and certainly showed no willingness to put it on public display, Bob Frame was also a decent singer with a particular penchant for Scottish ballads. With a fair prevailing wind, he might just be persuaded to go public once a year on Hogmanay.

The Palace was about ten minutes' walk from Bulmer Street, by way of Strawberry Place, a right turn into Leazes Park Road and a left on to Percy Street. The night was, by the recent standards of October weather, pleasantly dry and mild as the foursome made their way to the theatre. With time on their hands, they decided to call in at the Percy Arms for a pre-theatre drink. They found a table for four in the relatively quiet lounge bar on the first floor and while Bob got the ladies settled into their seats, Harry made his way to the bar counter to order the drinks. As he waited for his two halves of best scotch, a gin and lime and a port and lemon, he glanced in the mirror behind the barmaid, which stretched the length of the bar and offered a good view of the whole room.

To his immense surprise, his attention was drawn to a table in the corner which was occupied by none other than Danny Veitch, Gordon Hugill and Betty Forster. This was becoming a habit! To all intents and purposes, they were enjoying a quiet and innocent drink together. It was only one night after Mary Bartlett's funeral and it was quite plausible that Gordon and Betty, probably at Betty's instigation, had invited Danny out so that he had some company at what was a difficult time for all three of them. On the other hand, this was the third time in five days he had seen Hugill and Veitch together which certainly gave the lie to Hugill's claim that they were not 'big mates.' This was food for thought at the very least, especially in light of Bob's assertion that he had a niggling feeling that there was more to Gordon Hugill than met the eye.

It was apparent that none of them had noticed Harry who, in any case, had other priorities. This was not the time to make his presence known; they did not want to be late for the show and he had no good reason to approach them in any case. Picking up the tray of drinks, he made his way unobtrusively back to the table. He made no comment on the situation, but he would certainly make Bob aware of the brief sighting the next morning. His reaction would be interesting and Harry himself was becoming increasingly persuaded that there was no smoke without fire.

Meanwhile it was a matter of drinking up and completing their journey to the Palace. The show must go on.

CHAPTER TWELVE

THURSDAY, 11TH OCTOBER

MATILDA ARNOTT and Albert Whittaker had been courting for eighteen months. Albert was a bank clerk at a prestigious branch on Grey Street, the finest street in the city, in the centre of Newcastle. His place of work was a short distance from the Theatre Royal which, together with nearby Grey's Monument, presented a magnificently imposing focal point in the town centre.

The Monument was completed in 1838, having been paid for by public subscription in recognition of Prime Minister Charles Grey's role in the passing of the Great Reform Act of 1832. Grey was a local man who had been born in Alnwick and the impact of his government's Reform Bill was felt throughout the country. It brought about the elimination of many anomalies, irregularities and downright wrongs in the electoral system and was acclaimed as a landmark piece of legislation. The local man who designed the figure of Earl Grey, Edward Bailey, was also responsible for the figure of Lord Nelson in Trafalgar Square.

Albert knew in his heart from their first meeting that he and Matilda were destined for each other. He was a man of foresight, as well as having a professional understanding of the value of saving and almost from day one he began putting money aside for the engagement ring which he hoped and believed would one day adorn her finger. Matilda had so many obvious charms in Albert's eyes, which made him achingly aware of his good fortune in making such a fine catch. She was distinctly pretty and petite and possessed a sweet nature. She had a pleasing level of innocent sophistication and mixed well. She was an accomplished cook and enjoyed entertaining. The pair also had a number of interests in common. For instance, they were enthusiastic and reasonably accomplished badminton partners and enjoyed the discipline of ballroom dancing. They were keen theatregoers who regularly attended the Theatre Royal, and they took great pleasure in dining out together.

If Albert was passionately in love with Matilda, and he certainly was, she was equally enamoured of Albert. She thought him handsome, with his sturdy good looks, his affable nature and his unfailingly considerate treatment of her. She regarded him as a decent man and someone she could trust. They were relaxed and happy in each other's company and were regarded by their friends as an ideal couple.

Matilda's career as a primary teacher at the local suburban school in Jesmond was a consuming and devoted passion. She was conscientious and she had a winning way with the children in her care; another virtue which was not lost on Albert. Her spare time spent in Albert's company was equally treasured. He was a steady, reliable, pleasant young man with good career prospects. Already there had been talk of him becoming bank manager material in the coming years.

In short, they were an idyllic couple and their relationship enjoyed the enthusiastic approval and support of both families. It was regarded as a matter of time before Albert made the customary formal approach to Mitchell Arnott, Matilda's solicitor father, in order to seek his daughter's hand in marriage.

Albert and Matilda had both been saving assiduously against the day when they were able to announce their engagement. They had set their sights on a pleasantly suitable house in the fashionable suburb of Jesmond, which fell marginally within their budget and upon which they intended to place a deposit. Their minds were increasingly exercised by the setting of the date for their engagement and, following much discussion and deliberation, they had eventually settled on 30th October. This was Matilda's birthday and while they had given a great deal of thought to dates nearer to Christmas, these had finally been rejected. They felt, somewhat selfishly they both agreed, that the nearer the date they selected was to the festive period, the greater was the potential for competition from, and even clashes with, other seasonal activities. There would, after all, need to be an engagement party to which all their friends would have to be invited. Besides, Matilda had warmed to the idea of walking down the aisle of St. George's Church with Albert on her arm on her birthday. Albert, frankly, would have been content to walk down the aisle with Matilda as his companion on any day of the year!

The date having been set, Albert sought a meeting with Mr. Arnott and asked permission to have his daughter's hand in marriage. Mr. Arnott consented with alacrity. Mrs. Arnott cried, the prospective bride and groom hugged and kissed each other, and all was well with the world.

Before an official announcement could be made, there was the not inconsiderable consideration of Matilda's engagement ring to be taken into account. Key to Albert's strategy in saving as much as he could from the earliest days of their courtship had been to accumulate enough money to place a deposit on a house, but this was a relatively small consideration when compared with the cost of the engagement ring. He had been determined to have enough money to buy Matilda a ring which would do her justice. It would also be required to be of such a price and quality as to show wholehearted commitment to their relationship, to say nothing of impressing Matilda's friends and colleagues, as well as making them green with envy.

The happy couple having decided on the date of the engagement, the process of choosing the ring began in earnest. They were searching for a ring which not only fell within Albert's not inconsiderable budget but they both knew it would need to be a gem which would match the sparkle in Matilda's eyes. It also needed to be sufficiently visually appropriate to reflect the depth of Albert's love, devotion and generosity.

Albert pronounced himself entirely content to leave the actual decision to Matilda who, for her part, had set her heart on a diamond solitaire. She was, of course, hoping her choice would meet with her future husband's approval as much as it did hers, though secretly she had every confidence in her feminine powers to win him over, should the need arise.

After an increasingly tedious round of several jewellery stores, they eventually decided to discard all except two, which had ample ranges from which they felt their needs could be met. They gave their devoted attention first, therefore, to the showroom windows of Northern Goldsmiths, the jewellers which had stood on the corner of Blackett Street for 150 years and which enjoyed an impeccable reputation. The other runner in the frame was Mickler and Goldberg's jewellery store in the Grainger Market which, in its ten years of existence, had become a minor mecca of quality and fashion with a particular appeal for young people.

Eventually they crossed the Rubicon. Matilda and Albert set their sights on a ring they actually wanted to try on. It was on display in the window of Mickler and Goldberg's. They stepped into the store and approached the counter where a well-presented and genial man dressed immaculately in a blue serge suit and a muted grey tie, asked if he could be of service. Albert, being a man of methodical mind, as befits a bank clerk, had made a note of the number of the tray in which the ring nestled in the showroom window so temptingly, and this he presented to the assistant. Betty Forster, who would normally have attended to the enquiry, was busy with another customer. It transpired that the term 'assistant' when applied to the natty gentleman standing before Albert and Matilda was not in keeping with his status. Probably motivated by the price range of the rings in the tray and the well-to-do nature of the customers before him, he took it upon himself to reveal that he was actually Mr. Goldberg, one of the owners of the store. His business acumen told him that these people may be about to invest a substantial sum of money in one of his products. He sensed an opportunity and he was determined to exploit it himself, so a charm offensive involving one of the hierarchy of the business was the order of the day. So well it might be!

The ring in question carried a price tag of £1000. Enough to raise a gasp in the throats of most people. It was not a price routinely paid for an engagement ring. It was twice the price of a more than desirable house such as that which Matilda and Albert had their eyes on. However, it had to be admitted that it was not unknown by any means for members of a family possessing the middle-class aspirations of the Arnott's and the Whittaker's to consider such an investment. How could it be justified? At the end of the day it did not need to be. Albert had saved the money, though unbeknown to Matilda, he had received a decent supplement from his father. He wished for the best for Matilda and she should have it. The investment need not compromise their other financial commitments, for which they had set aside the appropriate funds. Whilst others may be envious; aghast even, it was his decision to make and his mind had been made up from the first. They had decided that when they were married, they would be known as Mr. and Mrs. Arnott-Whittaker and they meant to live in the style of a couple with such a fine sounding name.

Matilda spent some time examining the ring, first in the showroom tray and then with even greater devotion from a series of angles on her engagement finger. She stood in front of a nearby full-length mirror and wafted her left hand in front of her to assess the impact the ring would have on those of her friends who would gaze on it enviously. Albert made suitably encouraging and approving comments. Both parties were satisfied that the ring met all their criteria and they made their decision known to Mr. Goldberg. The jeweller was delighted. It was not every day they sold a ring of this price and he was anxious that things should proceed smoothly. Accordingly, he eulogised;

'Madam, it looks simply exquisite.' Mr. Goldberg, experienced as he was in these matters, knew he had the winning post in his sights, and he changed his strategy ever so slightly. He was a smooth operator if nothing else;

'Madam, I do assure you the ring looks simply divine, but if I may make so bold, it looks ever so slightly loose on your finger. I would suggest it would be a sensible precaution, should you choose to select it, for us to measure the circumference of your finger and make any necessary small adjustment to guarantee an absolutely perfect fit. This might also require some minor alteration to the positioning of the stone within the ring or a process of heating the ring and reducing its circumference.

'We have the expert services of our Mr. Simpson to carry out this kind of minor work and whilst it is routine, it does require precision. Mr. Simpson was trained in Hatton Garden and has considerable experience and expertise. This would, of course, incur no further expense on your part. The perfect fitting of a ring of this quality is something upon which any quality jewellery emporium would pride itself, and Mickler and Goldberg is no exception.

'If the gentleman would be willing to leave a modest deposit of five guineas to secure the sale of the ring, we would guarantee to have any adjustment completed within seven days and you could collect it a week today.'

Matilda and Albert were highly impressed by Mr. Goldberg's professionalism and saw the wisdom of having the minor fitting alteration carried out. Matilda would have liked to take the ring straight away but waiting a week for perfection seemed a sensible precaution. The ring was a lifetime investment. The agreed deposit was therefore paid. Mr. Goldberg took very great care to measure the circumference of Matilda's finger and finally all transactions were completed.

The young couple thanked Mr. Goldberg for his kind assistance and all three were beaming profusely as Matilda and Albert left the shop, while a very contented Goldberg placed the ring in his safe. It was a supremely happy pair that stepped out of the Grainger Market to meet the sunny afternoon which perfectly matched their mood.

The task of making the adjustments to the ring fell to Israel Simpson. It was by no means the routine exercise Samuel Goldberg had outlined. All of Simpson's Hatton Garden expertise would be required and time was not necessarily on his side.

The relationship between Messrs. Mickler, Goldberg and Simpson was one which sought to take maximum advantage of situations such as this when they presented themselves. Honesty was not at its heart. What they were about to contemplate was to purchase an apparently duplicate but actually inferior stone and substitute it for the original. Simpson's task would be to identify such a stone and to alter it in such a way as to make it resemble the original as closely as possible, without the unfortunate purchasers being aware of, or able to recognise, any difference as a consequence of his actions.

Simpson's first task would be to take the ring to his workshop and carry out a thorough examination. He would not be looking for flaws, for there were unlikely to be any of even slight significance in such an expensive stone. He would be trusting his experience to tell him the characteristics of the stone in terms of design, shape and colour. The ring had been obtained from a highly respectable wholesaler and Simpson would be using his experience to absorb its characteristics.

However, a flawless stone is virtually unknown. It can contain so-called feathers, which are extremely difficult to detect. These are tiny cracks or fissures which are usually located deep in the stone. Simpson anticipated no such visible examples in Matilda and Albert's stone, but his knowledge of its characteristics would be essential in finding a duplicate. Matilda's ring contained its own subtleties. It was known as a "cushion cut" for example, so called because it superficially resembled the shape of a cushion or pillow. It was a solitaire ring featuring a single stone which radiates its sparkling beauty like no other in its natural light. Set in platinum and elegant in design, solitaire rings never date or go out of fashion. This feature was one of the many which had appealed to Matilda, who saw her engagement ring as a permanent and visible token of her love for Albert, and his for her.

For these reasons. Simpson would not be making any alterations to the original stone. The plain fact was, this would not be the stone the customers received when they returned in a week's time. The time spent studying its characteristics was, however, a crucial first step in the process. His next task was to take the ring to the wholesaler and search for a diamond which was as close in shape, colour, and design as possible. It would have to be flawed in one or more ways which would make it much less costly. He would then carry out such changes to the diamond as were necessary to complete the subterfuge, so that only a person with his experience and expertise, of whom there were very few, would be able to tell the difference.

So, what would he be looking for Flaws of the kind Simpson would find under microscopic examination were known as inclusions. These are slight irregularities which are taken into account when the value of the stone is being assessed. They would be visible to a skilled diamond grader under 10+ magnification and an expert of Simpson's skill and experience would attempt to minimise their impact by judicious cutting or polishing. Inclusions are the principal reason why a flawless diamond is exceptionally rare.

So, the original stone carefully concealed in his pocket, Simpson set off to visit the Yorkshire showroom where he hoped to find a suitable copy. He did so in a small car he had bought a year ago as a justifiable expense, as well as a personal indulgence, and which he used almost exclusively for these trips. He spent three hours on his quest comparing stones. This was the most critical part of the whole exercise and it was not until he was completely satisfied that the duplicate he had selected could be fashioned into a near-perfect copy of the original, that he regarded this part of his work as complete.

Delighted to have been able to find such a stone, he paid the asking wholesale price, pocketed the gem and left the premises. Satisfied with his work and suddenly aware that it was the middle of the afternoon and he had not eaten, he felt the need to assuage his hunger. He knew of a very pleasant restaurant quite close by, so he made his way straight there. He savoured a bowl of onion soup, a main course of roast chicken with new potatoes, broccoli, carrots and gravy and a dessert of his favourite crème caramel, as well as a handsome glass of wine. He paid the bill, strolled to his car and set off for Newcastle, whistling to himself in quiet satisfaction. It would be eight o'clock in the evening before he was home, but he was content that he, and his business partners Mickler and Goldberg, would soon be handsomely rewarded as a result of his diligence.

He had bought a legitimate though not perfect solitaire stone. Taking into account the wholesale profit margin, this was a saving of almost £500 when it was compared with the price of the stone in Matilda and Albert's ring. Of this money, his professional expertise entitled him to 25% under his arrangement with Mickler and Goldberg, who would share the balance.

When you consider the average tradesman's annual wage was £125 a year (or £2 ten shillings per week) and the asking price of a house such as that being contemplated by Matilda and Albert was £500 and when you take into account Simpson's new car has cost £300 a year ago, Simpson and Mickler and Goldberg's return on the transaction represented a very hefty profit. He would be picking up in excess of a year's wages for his efforts and whichever way you looked at it, that was a substantial sum of money. This, as they say, was the life.

Simpson then spent best part of two days working on the duplicate stone, even giving some small jobs from the growing backlog of his routine shop repair work to Gordon Hugill to deal with at a small spare work bench next to his own, to ease the pressure. After a final polish and close examination of the finished product, he was happy that his work measured up to his usual standard. He, therefore, completed the exchange of the duplicate for the original in the platinum ring and his work was done. How long, he wondered, before the next opportunity presented itself It might be four weeks or six but for sure the work would keep coming.

Israel Simpson was not by nature an extravagant man like Davy Conlon. He allowed his natty dressing to be a usefully distracting talking point among the market people. It suited him to have the persona of a slightly eccentric individual as it meant people tended to leave him to his own devices. However, he had a very healthy savings account. Despite having told the police he had moved to the North East to marry the woman he loved, he was actually a bachelor, who had created the fiction for reasons of his own. He had no family to provide for and he was a man of genuine substance. He was also, for the present, a man of few self-indulgences. There would be time for those when he felt he had enough money to give up his current way of life. He had already planned the kind of pleasant retirement which awaited him when his bank balance had reached the target he had set himself, and he calculated that in two years he would be able to call it a day and begin his new life of leisure.

Meanwhile, after seven days which had contained more than their share of trembling impatience and eager anticipation, Matilda and Albert almost ran through the double doors of Mickler and Goldberg's Jewellery showroom to be met by Mr. Samuel Goldberg. He was his usual effusive self.

'Ah, Mr. and Mrs...oops, forgive me. Not quite yet! I am getting a little ahead of myself. It is a very clear step in that direction, however.'

Goldberg stood with a far from sincere looking grin plastered on his face. A little of his ingratiating charm went a long way;

'I am assuming you are here to collect your lovely ring?' he said rhetorically. 'Excuse me while I fetch it from the safe.'

This brought normality to the situation, as well as smiles all round. Mr. Goldberg excused himself while he went to bring the object in question, returning to hand over the neat and unobtrusive jeweller's box in which it was nestling. Matilda just about managed to contain her desire to snatch it and run, and instead opened the box to remove the ring. She allowed Albert to place it on her ring finger and they both drooled.

Matilda was in raptures;

'It's absolutely divine, It fits like a glove as it were, ha, ha!'

A now controlled Samuel Goldberg advised Matilda to

be satisfied with every aspect of Mr. Simpson's work as he returned the original deposit of five guineas to Albert. He in turn handed over a certified cheque for £1,000 from his bank. Matilda was still euphoric; 'Oh, thank you so much, Mr. Goldman,' she gushed, 'It's perfect. Please thank Mr, Simpson for us.'

'Thank you, Miss. It has been a delight doing business with you both and on behalf of Mr. Mickler and myself, not forgetting Mr. Simpson, of course, may I take the opportunity to wish you a wonderful married life together.'

He was tempted to suggest they may like to come back nearer the time to select their wedding rings, but he decided not to press his luck. He was content to assure the young couple that Mickler and Goldberg would always be there to assist them in the future should the need arise. It was not exactly the subtlest of hints, as Goldberg imagined it to be, but he was confident that things would take their course.

Once again, there was geniality all round, though Goldman's obsequious grin came more from his lips than from his heart. The morning's business was concluded. Once more Matilda and Albert left the premises arm-in-arm, wreathed in smiles, while Mr. Goldberg made for the safe into which he deposited Albert's cheque. Then he locked the safe and allowed himself a small smile of satisfaction. This time it was heartfelt.

CHAPTER THIRTEEN

THURSDAY, 11TH OCTOBER

HARRY MAGUIRE and Bob Frame were holding a two-man conference in their office at Market Street police station. It would be taking things too far to suggest that the investigation was stagnating. They still had a prime suspect in Davy Conlon, but they were no nearer uncovering the crucial evidence which would bring the case to a conclusion.

Major crimes are sometimes solved by a slice of luck, a careless word or an unexpected coincidence, though DC Bob Frame would tell you there is no such thing as coincidence. What could be the breakthrough sometimes came from an unlikely source or a previously overlooked piece of evidence. Harry and Bob would prefer to solve the murder of Mary Bartlett by their own skill and intellect, but they would not be averse to a lucky break from whatever source. They were still faced with a number of imponderables, and they felt the need to go over the evidence as it stood and decide on their next move.

Bob Frame being the sort of meticulous individual he was, opened the discussion with a detailed summary of where they stood;

'What do we have to go on? We have a chief suspect who was with the victim a matter of minutes before she was killed. He had attempted to sexually assault her, and she had rejected him vigorously, threatening to tell her boss – his wife – as well as her boyfriend, what had taken place. He needed to keep her quiet. Is that not motive enough? He certainly had opportunity, but we need to find a knife which he could have used. We need to prove that he stabbed her. Without those pieces of evidence our case is circumstantial and will not stand up in court.

'We also have to ask ourselves whether he was physically capable of carrying or dragging the corpse to the shop where it was found. Then there is the matter of the blood. The only way I can see there was no blood on the ground from her stab wound would be if she was wrapped in something. A sheet or a blanket for instance. There is no sign of anything like that in the shop and I cannot see where he would have either the time or the opportunity to hide something bulky like that or dispose of it. Unless he had an accomplice, which is virtually impossible given the fact that he claims he was alone with her in the shop. The more we look at it, the less likely it becomes that Conlon was the murderer.

'I know he fits, but there are too many unknown factors. If we can't find the weapon, or the cloak or whatever it was, either he is going to get away with it, or he did not do it.'

Bob's tone was downbeat as he came to the end of his summary. If he was to be honest, he was feeling less and less confident that Davy Conlon was their man, but if he did not do it, who the Hell did? Harry sounded exasperated as he replied;

'I still think Conlon is favourite, but I have to agree with your analysis. I am ruling out the possibility of an accomplice. It simply isn't viable. We are missing something, Bob, and for the life of me I cannot see what it is. If it is not Conlon, then, unfortunately, we are virtually back at the beginning.'

They decided to go down to the canteen and have a cup of tea. It usually helped. Half an hour later, with two biscuits and a cuppa each inside them, they returned to the office where Harry resumed the conversation by coming from a different angle;

'I want to speak to Hugill and Veitch again. Those two are up to something, I am convinced of it. They could well know something they are keeping to themselves.'

'It might be a decent shout to have then in again, I agree,' Bob replied. 'Whatever they like to tell us to the contrary, they are as thick as thieves. It may not have a direct bearing on the case, but we have to get to the bottom of what they are up to with these hole-in-the-corner meetings of theirs every five minutes. We might as well have another go at Conlon while we are at it. It is time we rattled his cage again. He has had plenty of time to sweat. The trouble is, we have nothing new to put to him, plus, if he does come in again, he is sure to have his brief with him. Let's face it, we are going around in circles. We need a lucky break.'

They decided to speak to Danny Veitch and Gordon Hugill separately and they were about to send PC Lloyd to fetch Veitch when there was a knock on the door. Young PC Lloyd stepped in and spoke apologetically;

'Excuse me, Guv. Sorry to disturb you both, but there is

someone here to see you.'

'Oh, and who might that be, Constable?'

'It's Danny Veitch, Sergeant.'

Bob and Harry were flabbergasted.

'This is bizarre, Bob. And you say there is no such thing as coincidence. What on earth can he want? Surely not to confess!'

'I haven't the foggiest,' Bob replied.

Harry turned to PC Lloyd;

'Very well, Show him in, lad.'

Danny was not exactly his brash and brazen self. He looked like a young man with something on his mind. Harry's thoughts went back to the incident in the Trent House when Danny had appeared to have something to say, then changed his mind. Was this the next step? Had he decided to get whatever it was off his chest?

Maguire would soon know;

'Come in, Danny. Have a seat. What can we do for you?'

Harry decided the friendly approach was best in the circumstances. He had no idea what had brought Danny in, and he was intrigued. He wanted to hear what the young man had to say for himself and he had no wish to appear hostile.

Danny came straight to the point:

'I know you think I am a bit of a lad, Mr. Maguire, but as I told you, I am law-abiding.'

Harry could not resist;

'Never mind the bullshit, Danny. What is this all about?'

'Well, I know you have seen me with Gordon Hugill a few times lately. I saw you looking at us in the Percy the other night when you thought I hadn't noticed, and there was the night at the boxing. Gordon told me you asked him about it when you interviewed him. I expected you would want to talk to me again, so I have taken the bull by the horns and decided to let you know what is going on.'

'You are quite right, Danny. For a couple of blokes who claim not to be close, you seem to be spending a lot of time in each other's company. It would not be a problem in normal circumstances. You are perfectly entitled to knock around with whoever you like and neither of you have ever been in trouble with the police, but these are not normal circumstances. I am sure you can understand our curiosity.'

'The point I want to make, Mr. Maguire, is that Gordon is not as thick as he seems. People think he is slow because he stutters, but he isn't. He likes to play on it as well, so that people underestimate him. He is actually quite bright, and he is also a devious bugger. He watches what is going on to see if he can exploit it. Take his work at the jewellers. He pretends he is slow and can just do basic repairs, but he is always reading stuff about gold and platinum and diamonds and that. He watches that Jewish bloke, Simpson, in his workshop like a hawk and knows far more than he lets on.'

Bob Frame was taking all this in. He realised that if what Danny was saying was true, it underlined his own opinion that there was more to Gordon Hugill than met the eye. Harry also sensed the possibilities in what Danny was claiming and he pressed on, encouraging the lad to say more. His instincts had told him previously that Danny was not just the brash youngster people took him to be, but that he had a quick mind and what he was saying was potentially useful;

'This could be valuable information, Danny. Is it connected with the sudden rush of meetings between the pair of you?'

'Yeah. He seems to have cottoned on to me since Mary was killed. I thought at first it was because the four of us had been hanging about together and we were upset by what had happened. That's a part of it, of course, but these last three times he has sought me out. He couldn't say much the other night because Betty was with him, but at the boxing and another couple of times he was talking about some business at the jewellers where he works.

'He had two ideas and he was angling for me to join him. First up, he reckons the security at Mickler and Goldberg's is not too clever. He seems to think it would be possible to pinch the odd item from time to time and it wouldn't be noticed. He was trying to find out whether I would know anyone who could fence things, and he said he would cut me in for a share. I am not a thief, Mr. Maguire, and I told him I wasn't interested.

'Then he started going on about how he thought that bloke Simpson was bent. He did not go into details. I don't think he knows exactly what is going on, but he reckoned Simpson was either fiddling for himself or in cahoots with Goldberg and Mickler in some scheme. He seemed to be thinking about blackmailing Simpson into letting him in on the action, but he needed to find out exactly what was happening before he could make a move. I told him I wanted nothing to do with it. I thought you should know about it, though. It's got nowt to do with the murder, but

Gordon is convinced there is something criminal going on.'

This was fascinating. Harry realised that while what Danny was saying was speculative, there seemed to be more than a possibility there was something behind it. His revelations about Gordon Hugill were also significant. Harry was inclined to pursue the matter if he could find some more tangible evidence. Any link with the murder seemed very unlikely to say the least, but these people were all connected in some minor way. His instinct was that Danny Veitch could be useful had been confirmed by what he had revealed and if there really was something out of order taking place at the jeweller's, having Danny on the inside could prove to be a major bonus. Harry decided he had no choice but to chance his luck;

'Danny, what you are telling me has the potential to be very useful and important. You will realise that I would need firmer evidence before I could take any direct action. Would you be prepared to string Gordon along and pretend you might be interested? If he was to come up with something more concrete to go on, you could let us know and we could investigate. How do you feel about that?'

'Well, Mr Maguire, I wondered whether you would ask me that and it was the main reason why I hesitated before deciding to come and see you. I'm not a criminal as I say, but I am not a snitch either. What I will do is go along with this and see where it leads, but I'm not going to get myself involved in anything iffy, and I won't push Gordon to tell me what he is up to. On the other hand, if he lets me know there is something definitely criminal going on, I'll pass it on to you. That's as far as I am prepared to go.'

'That's fair enough, Danny and I appreciate it. I won't press you for information, but I will take seriously anything you do come up with. I need to warn you to take care. If this is big, the people involved may well be dangerous. I know this is not your style but as you say, if there is something big in the offing, we need to know. Keep in touch. You only need to say we have pulled you in for more questioning if anyone sees you coming in here.'

That was the arrangement which both sides settled for and Danny went on his way. Bob and Harry needed to analyse what had just taken place.

'What about it, Bob? Is this just a distraction we could do without, or do you think it is worth our time and attention?'

Bob was clear about his reaction;

'We have to go along with it if he does come up with anything. I don't see a link with the Bartlett murder, but preventing another crime which is close to the case would do us no harm. Besides, you never know when one thing might lead to another. I must admit he seemed sincere enough and I have no reason not to believe what he told us. You know I have had my doubts about young Hugill, and it is encouraging to have been confirmed in my opinion. Whether he turns out to be a master criminal or a brilliant jewel thief I doubt, frankly, but if he is getting himself involved in the beginnings of something out of his depth and Danny can give us the inside track, well and good.'

CHAPTER FOURTEEN

SATURDAY, 13TH OCTOBER

THERE WAS another major surprise for Harry Maguire and Bob Frame when Danny Veitch appeared at the police station at around midday the following morning. They had decided to put in another shift despite it being the weekend as they continued their search for the breakthrough in the Mary Bartlett case which had so far eluded them. They remained convinced of Veitch's genuineness and if he was paying them a return visit so quickly, it could only mean either there had been a new development or the whole idea had gone down the drain. There was no likely middle ground.

Danny had called during his lunch break and he was consuming the remnants of a sausage sandwich as PC Lloyd ushered him into the office.

'Hello again, Danny,' Detective Sergeant Harry Maguire greeted the young man he was beginning to regard as something of a protégé.'

'Good morning, Sarge,' Danny replied breezily,''I just thought you would like to know Gordon Hugill came to see me after work last night and we went to have a drink at his suggestion. He reckoned Simpson had been away on business on Thursday. Apparently, he had been to Yorkshire visiting the jewellery wholesale place where they buy their trays of jewellery and individual items. Gordon says he had been cagey about why he had been away when he came back to work yesterday, but he would not have driven all that way unless it was important. Simpson was already in his workshop when Gordon arrived for work. He was working on a ring and he gave Gordon some repairs to get on with and sat him at the spare bench beside his own.

'Simpson became engrossed in his work and did not speak, concentrating 100% on the stone he had under his microscope. Gordon eventually asked him what he was doing, and Simpson replied that he was doing a bit of cutting and polishing on a stone he had bought at the wholesaler's. Gordon said he had a smile on his face as if he was pleased with himself and when he had finished his work, he put the stone in a platinum ring and clasped it. Then he put the ring in a small presentation box. He said he was going across the market to see Mr. Mickler and Mr. Goldberg and would be back in about an hour. He went out of his shop whistling a tune and told Gordon to keep an eye on things until he came back.

'Gordon wasn't very happy because he doesn't like dealing with the public on account of his stutter, so he asked if Betty could come across from the main shop to cover. Sure enough, she appeared about ten minutes later, but the place was quiet. The two of them got on talking and Betty said Mickler and Goldberg were in what she called a skittish mood as if something good was happening. Betty is not one to be nosey, Mr. Maguire, but she overheard them talking about some young couple's engagement ring. She had been standing behind a fixture showing a woman a bracelet and the two of them were ignoring her.

'Apparently she heard Goldberg say something like "those two stuck up so-and-so's won't notice the difference in a hundred years. Simpson may be a bit volatile and unpredictable but there is no-one to touch him when it comes to cutting and polishing stones. The new stone will look just like the original. You know, he's done it before often enough." Then she heard Mickler mutter something about them having him over a barrel anyway and he would not dare to try and pull a fast one on them.

'Betty's customer decided she would like to see something else, so she had to go and get it out of the showroom window, so that was all she heard. She's a trusting lass and she probably wouldn't think too much about it, but Gordon said it was obvious they were working a fiddle. I don't know anything about the jewellery trade, but Gordon claimed there had been an odd occasion when a jeweller had been caught substituting a quality stone with an inferior one and pocketing the extra profit. Gordon reckons it's very hard to make a stone look better than it is, but maybe this Simpson bloke is one of the few people who can do it.'

Harry interrupted to give Danny a chance to catch his breath, as he had been rattling through his story;

'Let me be absolutely clear about this, Danny. Are you saying someone has bought a ring for a particular price then Simpson has made a replica from an inferior stone and replaced it?'

'That's what Gordon thinks. He's not certain, but he has

been reading up on ways in which jewellers have been done for this kind of thing and he thinks it is possible, especially with Simpson on board.'

'Danny, that is brilliant. You may have put us on to something major here. Diamond rings cost a fortune and swapping the stone could be very lucrative. Leave it with us and we will get on to it straight away.'

'That's okay, Sergeant. Glad to be of help. Do you want me to stay on the case, then?'

'Only if he raises the subject. Do not try to probe as I have said before. If this is true, there is huge money involved and if these people think you are snooping it could be serious for you. Step down if you want to, but if you are happy to carry on, for goodness sake watch your step.'

While PC Lloyd came to collect Danny to see him off the premises so he could return to work, Harry and Bob took stock of this potentially sensational new development. Harry began, as he so often did, by asking Bob for his opinion;

'What do you reckon, Bob? This sounds like it could be a really big deal.'

'Could be. I am like you, I know nothing about this kind of thing, but we need to talk to someone who does. I have a pal in the Fraud Squad who might be able to help. Do you want me to have a word with him?'

'Absolutely. You go and have a chat with your mate and get back to me. I will run the whole thing past the Spectre and see what he has to say. I will probably have to convince him there is the likelihood of some sort of connection with the Mary Bartlett killing, I expect. I am not at all sure there is a link or what it might be, but I will think of something. Besides, if he thinks there is a chance that we can hand him two major results he will probably snatch our hands off. You know what he is like.'

Having agreed that Harry would meet the Chief Superintendent on Monday morning, while Bob chased up his Fraud Squad connection, they called it a day.

CHAPTER FIFTEEN

MONDAY, 15TH OCTOBER

As arranged, Harry made straight for the office of Chief Superintendent Walton when he arrived at the Station on Monday morning, while Bob went to seek out his colleague in the Fraud Squad.

When Harry put the story that Danny Veitch had told him to his superior, the Chief Superintendent's initial reaction was one of scepticism. His first priority was a swift conclusion to the murder enquiry. He was not keen on the possibility of any sideshow which might cause a distraction. His instruction was for them to keep an eye on any developments, but he was basically lukewarm;

'Come back to me if you can come up with a genuine link to the Bartlett murder in the next twenty four hours; otherwise hand it over to the Fraud Squad.'

Harry understood the Chief's position. They were tasked with finding a killer. He had no choice but to comply, though knowing Bob Frame, if there was a connection between the two, he would come up with it, so in that sense, it was business as usual. He was happy to wait for Bob to report back after meeting his colleague in the Fraud Squad, hoping he would be able to verify the viability of what Danny Veitch was claiming.

Bob made a beeline straight for his pal, Don McCowey, and asked him for his take on the matter;

'I have been involved with fraud in the jewellery trade on more than one occasion,' Don said. 'I would not say it was widespread. Like most professionals, jewellers are honest people who take a pride in their work. However, there are some bad apples in every business and high-end jewellery sees a lot of money change hands. There is a level of temptation there and an unscrupulous person who possesses the necessary skills can make a fortune, believe me.

'I remember about seven or eight years ago there was a spate of the sort of corruption you are describing in London. It stands to reason that is where it could happen because Hatton Garden is the heart of the jewellery industry. If anyone had the necessary skills, that was where they could be found. No-one was ever caught, though, and it ended as abruptly as it had started. The word was that the net was closing around the guy who was responsible and he went to ground.'

'Mmm...were there any names in the frame?' Bob asked.

'Nobody firm, but as I have explained there was only a handful of diamond cutters who had the necessary skill to replicate a stone using an inferior one, and not many disappeared from the scene around that time. There is an outside chance that the work was being farmed out to one of the diamond centres in Europe, but I doubt it myself. The London trade is very much a closed shop. One of the main suspects actually died about a month after the scam came to a halt, and that dampened down the search to a certain extent.

'There were a couple of others who dropped out of sight. One was a bloke called Reuben Silverman and the other was a young whizz kid whose name was Watson or Wilson. It was alleged that Silverman went to Antwerp, which would make sense because it is one of the major centres of the trade in wholesale gold and diamonds in Europe.

'There was another rumour that he had been working for some really dubious individuals and he went to Australia to get away from them. Either way he was never seen again and, in any case, there was no solid evidence against him. He did have a reputation for having a bit if a short fuse and was capable of violence at the drop of a hat but, again, there was nothing tangible that could be pinned on him.

'The young chap is more likely to have stayed in the trade. He was a real chancer with a high opinion of himself. He certainly has not showed up in this country unless he is working in the shadows cutting diamonds to order for dodgy jewellers. Other than those three, there have been no reports that I have seen of the same sort of thing going on now, and the trail has been cold for years.'

Bob thanked his mate for the information, but neither he nor Harry was particularly enthusiastic or optimistic. One dead, one in Australia and one too young to match Simpson's profile did not give rise to much hope.

'That is disappointing to say the least, Bob,' Harry concluded dejectedly, 'I was hoping we were on to something there, but it doesn't look like it.'

Bob had a habit of taking a more pragmatic view. Harry

was the younger and less experienced man who was inclined to see things in black and white, while Bob's greater experience told him that things were seldom as they seemed. He was always prepared to look at the bigger picture and to consider more unlikely options;

'Not unless this Silverman individual did not actually go to Australia. Is there a possibility he put that rumour about, but he came up to these parts instead? He could have opened a modest business in the Grainger Market, don't you think? He was not known outside of London and if he changed his name as well that would give him a low enough profile. No-one would suspect.'

Harry was intrigued by Bob's reasoning;

'That's a possibility, I suppose. Is there any chance you could get in touch with your mate again and give him a description of Simpson? Tell him about his intelligence and his suave style and see if there is any possibility he could be Silverman.'

Bob got straight back to Don McCowey at the Fraud Squad. It seemed at first as though he would not be able to help. Silverman was described as nondescript; as a loner who kept himself to himself. He was not reckoned to be flamboyant by any stretch of the imagination. However, Don then made reference to an incident which Bob seized upon. Apparently, rumour had it that Silverman had been the victim of an attempted attack on his way home from Hatton Garden after work one night, but he turned on his would-be assailant with a knife and inflicted a nasty wound.

The attacker was known to the police but made no official complaint. He claimed not to know the name of the intended victim, who had knifed him and then ran off. He was, therefore, unable to press charges. Silverman also denied being attacked. His version of events was that a stranger approached him in a hostile manner demanding money. Silverman had taken to his heels and left the man in his wake. Neither story was believed, but in the absence of any witnesses the case was dropped.

Neither Bob nor Harry was prepared to dismiss the rumour, however flimsy the link might be. Harry was particularly enthusiastic;

'Now we might be getting somewhere. That knife incident could introduce a whole dimension if it is true. Silverman could not have been that nondescript if he was capable of knifing someone on the spur of the moment like that. We need to speak to Simpson again soon but first, I vote we go and see Mickler and Goldberg. If there is anything in this jewellery swindle allegation of Veitch's, we need to know how heavily involved they are and just what the set-up between the three of them is. Walton gave us twenty four hours to sort it, so we will make it our priority until then. They will certainly be able to shed some more light on Simpson, and there just might be a tie in with the murder.

'What I suggest we should do is to put it to the pair of them that we have information to the effect that a substitution has taken place involving a ring purchased from their premises. We can demand the names and addresses of the purchasers and say we are prepared to advise their insurers to have the ring examined by an expert. It might just be enough to put the frighteners on them. My guess is that if they have nothing to hide, they will be happy to co-operate, but if they are involved, they will try to point the finger at Simpson. Then we get them to tell us everything they know about him.'

Once again, Bob Frame felt the need to dampen down his guvnor's enthusiasm. The knife incident had been described by Don McCowey as a rumour. It was not evidence. He agreed that the course of action Harry was advocating had some merit, but it was not without risk;

'What if they call our bluff?'

'Well then, we do as we threatened and make the buyers aware of the information we have received and let them pass it on to their insurers, assuming they have had the wit to insure the ring. We will still have the right to question them regarding their knowledge of Simpson's background. Come on, let's get in touch and pay them a visit.'

'They will want to know where our information came from, which might put Gordon Hugill and Betty Forster in danger,' Bob reminded him.

'We will tell them we received it anonymously. They can figure it out for themselves. They might suspect their own staff or even each other. For our part, we can also suggest it was passed to us by the Fraud Squad who received it in connection with a separate investigation. I know we are taking a risk, Bob, but looking at what we stand to gain, it has to be worth it.'

Bob agreed the stakes were high, but he finally put his reservations to one side and the pair of them set off on the short walk to the jewellery shop, to cross swords with Mickler and Goldberg.

The two police officers were shown into a back room of the partners' premises. The two owners left Betty Forster to look after the counter, along with another older woman neither Bob or Harry recognised. Harry came straight to the point;

'Thank you for seeing us so promptly, gentlemen. As I think you are aware, we are investigating the recent murder of young Mary Bartlett, on which I can advise you we are making good progress. However, we are here to discuss a different matter. We need you to tell us all you know about Israel Simpson. What exactly is his position here? Is he one of your partners, an employee or a freelance jeweller who helps you out?'

`Mickler and Goldberg exchanged puzzled glances. Any initial apprehension they may have had faded somewhat with the realisation they were here to talk about Simpson rather than themselves, but they were not yet entirely relaxed. It was Mickler, who was rather more restrained and self-contained by nature than his partner, who answered;

'He occasionally does some specialist work for us as well as routine repairs. Mr. Goldberg and I buy our stock from the leading wholesaler in the North of England. We sell our jewellery to the general public from this showroom only. We are retailers, but we are not skilled jewellers who make pieces to order. Simpson has a small shop on the other side of the Grainger Market where he sells items of jewellery as well as watches. He also carries out any complicated repairs which are bought to us. Our apprentice, Gordon, spends most of his time in Simpson's workshop and carries out the more routine work. We hope he might be sufficiently skilled and experienced in due course to carry out all of our own repairs. That is the set-up in a nutshell, Sergeant. Essentially, we pay Mr. Simpson for his considerable expertise as and when we require it.'

Bob Frame picked up the questioning by asking; 'How did you become aware of Mr. Simpson?'

'He approached us a few years ago, when he opened up. He said he was an experienced diamond cutter and polisher and he would appreciate any work we were able to put his way.'

'Did you take up references?'

'No. We gave him a couple of tricky repairs and he carried them out to a high standard. It was obvious he knew what he was doing, and we took him at face value. Practical experience is the only reference you need in this business. All the work he has done for us has been first class.'

'Tell us what you know about his background and domestic situation, if you would.'

'The honest answer to that is not much. He lives quietly from what we can gather. He told us he came up North when he met a local girl, but he seldom refers to his home life. Neither of us has met Mrs. Simpson and he never makes reference to any children they may have.'

'Have you asked about him in the trade?'

'Not really. To be honest, we are happy with his work and we have no reason to pry into his background. It is not relevant. He seems to be a decent man. Occasionally flies off the handle but for the most part he is fine.'

This was proving to be a pat-a-cake interview so far, so Bob decided it was time to up the ante;

'Does the name Reuben Silverman mean anything to either of you, gentlemen?'

It was a question which clearly stunned both men. They blanched and looked across with involuntary glances in each other's direction. It was Goldberg who offered an unconvincing reply;

'No… that name does not ring a bell. Why do you ask?'

Samuel Goldberg was showing signs of agitation. There was perspiration on his brow, and it was obvious he was lying. He was attempting to buy time to gather himself, but Bob was having none of it;

'Come now, gentlemen. We are not fools and neither are you. We all know that Israel Simpson was formerly known as Reuben Silverman and he came to Newcastle after being suspected of fraudulent dealing in London. Let me come to the point. We have reason to believe, based on information from our colleagues in the Fraud Squad which they received in the course of a separate investigation, that Israel Simpson is involved in a serious crime.

'We believe he has substituted a solitaire diamond in a ring which was bought here and left on deposit for alteration. The substitute diamond is inferior and therefore much less costly. His expertise enabled him to remove or disguise imperfections from the inferior stone and the result was a substantial increase in the profit on the original transaction. That, gentlemen, is fraud. My question is simply this: what part did the pair of you play in this sordid and highly illegal transaction?'

It was obvious from the reactions of both men that they were beset by fear and guilt. There was no doubt in the minds of Maguire and Frame that the two jewellers were participants. They were in it up to their necks. Joshua

Mickler made a feeble attempt to deny all knowledge;

'He must have done this when he was examining the original stone for imperfections. That is standard practice when a diamond of this price is purchased.'

'Please do not insult our intelligence, Mr. Mickler, Harry cautioned, this was a task which we are informed required immense skill. 'We know that Simpson went to your wholesaler last week and bought a similar stone. It must surely have taken him a considerable time to remove the imperfections and carry out the exchange. I think the time has come for the pair of you to tell the truth. We are dealing with a very serious offence here.'

Harry was now confident that he had Mickler and Goldberg cornered. Their demeanour gave them away. They had no previous experience of having been interrogated by the police and their naivety showed. First had come the denial and now he anticipated that they would seek to place the blame for the entire fraud on Simpson. He leaned back in his chair and looked across at the pair of them, waiting for their next step. It was Goldberg who spoke. He was looking agitated and once again he took out a handkerchief to mop his perspiring brow before replying. What he had to say further vindicated Harry's approach;

'What you have to understand, officers, is that Israel Simpson is a very dangerous and unscrupulous individual. He was involved in violence in London and he has displayed volatile and unpredictable behaviour here. He had only been working for a few months in his shop when he approached us with the ring swapping idea. At first, we did not want to get involved, but he was insistent and made some very frightening threats towards ourselves and our families. We had no choice but to go along with his scheme.'

It was a nice try, but just what Harry had expected. Their strategy now was to shift the blame on to Simpson and paint themselves as the victims of circumstances. They knew they were in serious trouble and their guilt had shown in their responses to Harry's interview. He continued to press home his advantage;

'Let me remind you, Mr. Goldberg, that just a few minutes ago your colleague told us you had a routine business arrangement with Mr Simpson. He said you knew very little about his background or family life, that you had taken him on trust, and you had no reason to doubt him. Now you are describing him as the devil incarnate. A fiend who made threats to your families to coerce you into joining in his enterprise.

'If you and your family were being threatened in this way by a single individual, I can see no reason why you would not inform the police. Why would you decline the opportunity to report this man to the authorities? You say this arrangement has been going on since he first approached you about six years ago. No, gentlemen, it seems obvious to me that you jumped at the chance to make a fortune out of Simpson's scheme. The three of you have very obviously accumulated vast sums of money over that time. In fact, I will go further. It is my opinion that it was not Simpson who used pressure and threats to recruit you; it was the other way on.

'I believe you came to know about Simpson's background and his change of name. You then blackmailed him and threatened to reveal his whereabouts to certain people in London who were still interested in him. It is not you two who are living in fear of Israel Simpson, it is Simpson who cannot escape from your clutches. He is terrified of the hold you have on him and that is why he continues to work for you.'

Mickler and Goldman's body language now registered the hopelessness of defeat. They knew when to stop digging and realised it was time to serve their interests by putting matters on a legal footing. Mickler confirmed this by making the inevitable statement;

'Sergeant Maguire, Constable Frame, I am afraid Mr. Goldberg and myself have nothing further to say until we have consulted our legal advisers.'

'I think you are very wise,' Mr. Mickler,' and if I can give you a piece of sound advice, I would suggest you keep the contents of our conversation to yourselves until we have spoken to Israel Simpson.' 'After all,' he added, with more than a hint of sarcasm, 'as you say, he is a volatile and dangerous man! We will be talking to you again very soon. In the meantime, I have to tell you both that you are under arrest on suspicion of acting in a fraudulent manner and that anything you say will be taken down and may be produced in court. It is my intention to have you taken to the police station and held there pending further enquiries'

Mickler and Goldberg having been cautioned and placed under arrest, Bob and Harry remained on the premises as there was a strong possibility of them gathering together as much of their shop's stock as they could and absconding. The police could not afford to take any chances in what was bound to be a high-profile case. They must not allow the suspects to slip away. Bob grabbed the phone from the table and dialled Market Street Station, explaining the situation succinctly and asking for two officers to come immediately to Mickler and Goldberg's jewellery shop to pick up two suspects. The police were within their rights to do so as they had been charged with a serious offence. If necessary, Bob or Harry would make a plea before the magistrates when they were charged, that there was a serious security risk and the suspects should be remanded in custody.

Within ten minutes, a police van arrived and two uniformed constables duly hauled Mickler and Goldberg out of the store and bundled them without ceremony or dignity into the back of the van. Harry and Bob swept out of the room, through the jewellery shop showroom and returned without further ado to the Market Street Police Station.

The two of them were elated. The front-foot approach had worked like a charm and completely unnerved Mr. Goldberg in particular. He had folded like the proverbial pack of cards under their cross examination. They could barely contain themselves as they went to report the very real prospect of a major success to their Chief Superintendent. If they could now link Simpson to the Mary Bartlett affair in some way, which would not be easy but no longer seemed impossible, they would be home and hosed.

Their boss, Ken Walton, was every bit as delighted as they had anticipated, though he tried his best not to seem too jubilant and triumphal. The news his two young tyros had brought him vindicated his faith in them and the chance to bring the two jewellery fraudsters to justice would do wonders for his reputation, as well as enhance the kudos of his protegees.

The main prize still eluded them but, like Maguire and Frame, he was hoping they would be able to find a link to the murder investigation. What a superb triumph that would be. Maybe it was too much to hope for, but things were progressing well. Ken Walton could see his star rising in the firmament.

CHAPTER SIXTEEN

TUESDAY, 16TH OCTOBER

After their customary early morning cup of tea in the police canteen, Harry and Bob held their daily briefing on progress in the Bartlett murder investigation. Today's meeting was supplemented by time spent reviewing the previous day's sensational developments involving Messrs. Mickler and Goldberg, and their apparent collaboration with Israel Simpson in a jewellery fraud.

The two detectives outlined their plans for the next stage in the investigation, which was to interview and probably arrest Simpson, who had been accused by Mickler and Goldberg of being the actual perpetrator of the illegal change of diamond stones in a ring bought from their jewellery store in the Grainger Market. Supt. Walton was so buoyed by the state of things that he was happy for Harry and Bob to do the foot slogging and report back to him. It was a ploy which had worked very well so far, and he saw no reason to amend it.

'Go for it, lads,' he beamed,' and let us just get this business wrapped up. Leave the remand hearing to me. I will see to it that Mickler and Goldberg go nowhere.'

They knew it would not be as simple as that, and before

they set off to Simpson's shop, Maguire and Frame decided they should exchange views regarding the possibility of the scam being linked to the Bartlett murder. They already had a prime suspect in the person of Davy Conlon; their problem with him remained that, beyond circumstantial evidence, they were still short of a conclusive piece which would persuade a jury he was guilty. They knew they must still make that a priority unless something unexpected transpired when they spoke to Israel Simpson. They were still mindful that their wish to connect Simpson to the killing was hopeful rather than probable. Their consolation was that at least it was now an avenue they could justifiably explore before dismissing it outright.

Bob Frame began going through the rather tenuous strands of the Simpson connection;

'We knew from the outset that Simpson was in the vicinity of the crime scene. He actually came and told us himself he had been working late that night prior to going to his masonic lodge meeting with Davy Conlon. We have not yet given any serious consideration to the possibility of collusion between them. Is that a possibility? What do you think, Guv?'

'I am still not convinced. There is no sensible reason why the two of them would want to kill the girl. Simpson barely knew her, only as the girl from the nearby shop. He was not a close friend of Davy Conlon, or anyone else for that matter. They just happened to belong to the same masonic lodge and travelled together for their monthly meeting as a matter of convenience. There is no evidence to suggest that they socialised otherwise. Let's face it, they are as different as chalk and cheese. They just about had the time, but they certainly did not have the motive. As far as I am concerned it is a non-starter.'

'I can't dispute any of that,' Bob replied,' what it comes down to is whether Simpson himself had any reason to kill Mary Bartlett.'

'Once again, he had the opportunity. He was in the vicinity at the time, but I am struggling to find a motive. What reason would he have to kill her?'

'Let's work on the assumption that he had a motive, then, and see where it takes us.'

'Obviously, that would change the whole complexion of the investigation. It would allow is to take him seriously as a suspect.'

Bob was becoming irritated. They were going over old ground instead of approaching the matter from a different and more positive angle;

'Listen, Guv. If Simpson really is Reuben Silverman, which is looking more and more likely, that tells us he has previous for attacking someone with a knife and inflicting a nasty wound. That has to be given some weight.'

'Yes, but we still have to come down to motive. We still need a reason why he would be carrying a knife and why he would use it on the girl. I accept that he is the only person who might have been near her who possessed a knife. That is our sticking point with Conlon, but as far as Simpson is concerned it rules him in, not out.'

'Right, then let us work on a hypothesis outlining why he might do it.'

'It comes back to the fact that if this was a random killing.

he is not guilty, but if Mary Bartlett was in the wrong place at the wrong time, which is very possible, then he might have a motive.'

'Okay, then we have to link Mary's running and falling down somewhere adjacent to his shop, to her seeing something or hearing something serious enough for him to kill her. It's not likely but I suppose it is not impossible. I suggest we go and confront him with regard to the diamond swindle and at the same time ask him what more he can tell us about his movements on the night of the murder. He won't be as easy to deal with as Goldberg and Mickler were; he is far too clever and crafty for that. On the other hand, he might make a mistake if you can come up with one of your golden questions while he is concentrating on talking his way out of the jewellery business.'

They set off on the short walk from the police station to the Grainger Market. They entered the market by one of the Grainger Street entrances, where they were confronted by a hole in the ground which was roped off. Three workmen were peering into the hole with mild curiosity taking in the sound of banging and sawing. Nearby, a labourer was mixing a batch of cement. A languid looking bricklayer leaned against the wall with a cigarette dangling from his mouth. Harry produced his warrant card and asked him what was going on.

The artisan resisted the temptation to reply by saying; 'We are digging a hole, mate,' which he had already used several times that morning in response to the questions of curious passers-by. He seemed to think better of it when he considered he was talking to two coppers.

'They are digging tunnels in the basement,' was his more helpful reply. 'Nobody seems to know what they are for, but apparently they started digging them last year and we have been told to finish them. Some of the lads reckon they are putting tracks down for coal trucks but that is only guess work. If you really want to know, you should call in at the Market Superintendent's office. If anybody knows he should.'

Bob and Harry were intrigued, and although they had other pressing matters to attend to, they decided to take the bricklayer's advice. Any activity which could have a bearing on the murder needed looking in to and although the men had not been working on the tunnels when the murder occurred, the presence of existing work merited a brief investigation. If there were any tunnels, complete or otherwise, they might afford a useful entrance and exit to the ground floor for any assailant.

The Market Superintendent could shed no light on the purpose of the tunnels;

'Nobody is saying,' he confessed, 'and all we are hearing is rumours. We only work here. We are always the last to know,' he added sardonically.

He did, however, possess a set of plans showing the intended locations of the tunnels. Interestingly, there was one of them which more or less followed the path of Alley 3. This was the pedestrian route on which both the florist's and Simpson's shop were located. Bob and Harry asked if it was possible to see them, quoting the Mary Bartlett murder investigation as justification.

'You can if you think it would help, but I expect you will only see piles of rubble. The tunnels are nowhere near completed. Also, anyone wishing to go down there would need a set of keys to open the entrance door and only the foreman on the site and myself have those.'

Nevertheless, the two detectives asked to have a quick look and the Superintendent was happy to oblige. Thankfully, there was some crude overhead lighting to guide their way, but it soon became obvious that what they had been told was true. This particular tunnel was very much in its infancy and it was impossible to visualise anyone being able to navigate it. Unfortunately, the tunnel was, in every respect, a dead end.

Harry and Bob dusted themselves down as they clambered out the same way they had entered, and Harry was not slow to bemoan the fact that they would have to discount the tunnel as a possible escape route for Mary Bartlett's murderer.

'I suppose that was a worthwhile exercise, Bob,' he muttered in a disconsolate tone. 'It's a pity, though. That would have done us very nicely. No matter. Let's go and look up Israel Simpson.

Their route took them past the area of the market where the butchers plied their trade. It was a lively and bustling place. Men were at work carving, chopping and slicing at fresh animal carcasses, cutting them down into joints of meat and chops or putting lesser quality pieces through the mincer. There was plenty of noisy and good-humoured banter, as stall holders attempted to entice the customers who strolled between display counters assessing and comparing the size, quality, range and price of the meat on sale. Bob caught a brief site of Danny Veitch brandishing a meat cleaver with evident relish as he set about a rack of pork chops, but whether Danny was aware of their presence was hard to tell. He was certainly engrossed in his work and, in any case, they had no need or desire to interrupt him.

They had not previously visited Simpson's modest and frankly rather gloomy unit which bore the legend 'I. Simpson: Jewellery & Watches sold and repaired' painted in black on the lintel above the door. The single showroom window contained a small but tastefully displayed arrangement of men's pocket watches as well as both ladies' and gents' wrist watches. They were mostly modestly priced and included a selection of second-hand bargain items which were priced accordingly. The same criteria applied to the trays of jewellery displayed in the front of the window. Rings and bracelets were mostly of affordable quality and price and there was nothing at all to rival the top end ranges in the glaringly bright showroom windows of Mickler and Goldberg.

The detectives were about to enter the shop when Bob tugged at Harry's sleeve. Harry paused and turned, and Bob pointed wordlessly at the concrete market floor. Neither man spoke; instead, they slipped quietly into the next alley. They walked around the market, looking carefully at the floor for ten minutes, before they made an on-the-spot decision to take an early lunch. Only then would they seek out Israel Simpson.

The upstairs café in the Grainger Market was one of their favourite haunts on those days when they gave the distinctly average and uninspiring menu in the police canteen a miss. It provided particularly wholesome sausage and mash, which Harry ordered, while Bob was content to settle for a more modest but equally nourishing bowl of vegetable broth. This steaming delight came accompanied by a chunk of roughly cut fresh bread. As a concession to the time of day – it was barely half past eleven – they decided to forego dessert and contented themselves instead with a mug of strong tea which they lingered over until the large market clock registered the time at 12:30 on its imposing face.

The reason for this cloak and dagger activity and the beeline for the café, where they needed to gather their thoughts as well as satisfy their stomachs, was something Bob had noticed and drawn to Harry's attention. Something which might have a fundamental bearing on the Mary Bartlett murder case.

'How in Hell's name did nobody spot that?' exploded the normally temperate Harry Maguire. 'Bloody fools, that is what we are. Neither of us had the sense to take a look around the vicinity once we were assured there was no blood on the ground and nothing in the way of a weapon or traces of a struggle. Damnation!'

The cause of Harry's fury was the presence of a small iron grill which was set in the market floor just outside of Simpson's shop. It was similar in design to those which allowed rainwater to drain away from the street gullies outside, to prevent the roads from flooding. Their quick check had revealed that only a small number of units had similar gratings adjacent to them.

These grates provided a perfect means whereby it was possible for passers-by to have a restricted view into the basement where work might be taking place. They also afforded a modest amount of supplementary natural light from the main market area for anyone working in the basement. Most important in this case, the person in the cellar had an admittedly restricted view of the area immediately above them.

Harry was still fuming as he waited for his meal;

'We have missed a trick here, Bob. There are only a handful of these grills in the place, and therefore very few units with basements. This one is ideal for Simpson to work on his own undisturbed. More to the point, he could see something of what was going on at ground level. It would be a limited view; not very clear and not for very far, but he could certainly see.'

Bob was in agreement;

'Suppose this was the spot where Mary tripped and fell. Suppose Simpson was working in the cellar on another of his bogus rings. Suppose the clatter when she fell aroused his attention. She would be lying there, unconscious in the gloomy light. He thought she was spying on him and panicked. He slipped his knife into his pocket, grabbed a sheet or a curtain and a pair of gloves from his overcoat pocket, switched off the light and dashed upstairs. As Mary came around and was getting groggily to her feet, he grabbed her, wrapped the sheet around her and stabbed her. In the process, he recognised her as the flower shop girl. Suppose the shop keys fell from her pocket in the struggle. He picked them up, carried her to the shop, opened the door and placed her in the chair, before returning the keys to her pocket. Then he dashed back to his workshop, grabbed his coat and his masonic case and went outside to meet

Davy Conlon. He could easily have gone in early the next morning and disposed of the sheet, or whatever he had wrapped the girl in. I know that's a lot of supposes, but we now know he is a quick-tempered character and there was a hell of a lot to lose if the diamond scam was uncovered.'

'Why didn't he just switch off the basement light when he noticed her?'

'Good question. I think it is possible he simply panicked when he noticed her lying there. I'll bet she was face down and he had no idea how long she had been lying there before he noticed her. He would not have recognised her as the shop girl in the fading light. We now suspect that he owned a knife. Presumably he always kept it close by. Suppose he just grabbed it from a drawer and, acting on instinct, grabbed a sheet or whatever was at hand, raced up the stairs and killed her. We have said all along that the likeliest reason she was killed was because she was the victim of chance. This may be a long shot, Guv, but there are a lot of pieces here which could fit. Simpson is beginning to look like a better bet as the killer than Davy Conlon.

Harry was inclined to be persuaded. He certainly knew that their pending interview with Simpson had now taken on a different perspective. He and Bob agreed that their strategy now was to begin by confronting their man with the jewellery fraud then, when an opportunity presented itself, they would throw the murder in his direction;

'It might need one of your golden questions, Bob, but I think we could be close at last.'

Once they had eaten their meals and finished their mugs of tea, Det. Sgt, Maguire and Det. Const. Frame left the upstairs café, descended the stairs and made their way purposefully across the floor of the Grainger Market until they reached the door of Israel Simpson's shop once again. They were aware of the fact that they could be on the brink of the climax to their investigation. Most assuredly, the least they were likely to achieve was a confession from Simpson that he was a key player in the illegal substitution of an inferior stone in place of a high quality diamond solitaire.

It would be very satisfying to place him in a police cell alongside his cohorts Mickler and Goldberg, who at this precise moment were standing in the dock of the magistrates' court. Chief Superintendent Walton was making the case for them to be remanded in custody on a charge of being involved in a serious case of jewellery fraud. Bob and Harry knew they would need to remain focussed, particularly if they were to outwit Simpson in their attempts to prove any role he might have played in the death of Mary Bartlett. As the tinkle of the doorbell made known their arrival, both men subconsciously straightened their shoulders and held themselves at their maximum heights. They stepped into the small, gloomy shop and found Gordon Hugill and Betty Forster sitting on a small and well used sofa unwrapping their lunch. The shop was open for business but there were no customers to be seen. Harry greeted the courting couple and asked if the owner was on the premises.

'He is d-d-downstairs in the b-b-basement, Sergeant,' Gordon informed him, 'he has a tricky repair he is b-b-busy with.'

Harry and Bob opened the door behind the showroom counter which led to the basement. Bob led the way down the narrow, creaky wooden staircase and into the lower area.

'Good afternoon, Mr. Simpson,' Harry began, 'might we have a word?'

Simpson was concentrating on a bracelet which he had in front of him on his work bench. He was examining it through a magnifying glass which was attached to a clamp on the bench and he held a small jeweller's tool in his right hand. His attention was entirely on the job in hand and at the sound of Harry Maguire's voice he gave a startled gasp. Quickly regaining his composure, he laid down his working tool and turned to face his visitors. His expression was a combination of his usual urbane and self-contained self, and the merest hint of apprehension.

'Oh, good day, gentlemen. You startled me. How may I help you?'

Harry was not about to mince words;

'I will come straight to the point, Mr. Simpson. Your friends and associates Mr. Mickler and Mr. Goldberg are currently appearing in court facing serious fraud charges. We arrested them yesterday and we are here today to ask you to explain your role in the matter.'

Simpson gasped. He was clearly shocked and had not anticipated this line of enquiry and he seemed uncertain how to proceed. After a pause lasting several seconds, he played his first pawn;

'I will help you in any way I can, Mr. Maguire, but I assure you that I have no knowledge of this so-called fraud. I really do not know what you are talking about. If you could give me some more details maybe I could help.'

Harry swept aside Simpson's protests of innocence, which

he regarded as a play to buy himself some time to gather his thoughts;

'Mr. Simpson, we have information to the effect that you went to a jewellery wholesaler in Yorkshire last week where you purchased a diamond solitaire stone. This stone was inferior but, in most respects, identical in appearance to another stone of much higher value. This stone was in a ring purchased in Mr. Mickler and Mr. Goldberg's shop recently. You also took that stone to Yorkshire with you for purposes of comparison. We believe that you used your unique skills to cut and polish the inferior stone in such a way that it was, to all but the most skilful of observers like yourself, a replica of the original. You then substituted the inferior stone for the original and Mr. Mickler returned the ring to its purchasers. You and your two friends made a substantial and fraudulent profit as a result.'

Simpson had remained impassive throughout Harry's outline of the case against him and he made no reply.

'Have you anything to say in your defence, Mr. Simpson?'

The suspect maintained his silence.

'Then I must inform you that the evidence against you is conclusive. We have statements to support our case and we are most certainly in a position to arrest you. I am afraid you must expect to go to prison for a very long time. I also have to advise you that we will be questioning you regarding your possible involvement in another extremely serious matter.'

It may have been the realisation that he stood to face a custodial sentence, or possibly he had rightly interpreted the other 'extremely serious matter,' as being the murder of Mary Bartlett, but either way, Simpson's expression and his mood changed in the blink of an eye. The short fuse of which Harry and Bob had been made aware recently, manifested itself. His dark eyes took on a penetrating and menacing glare. He bared his teeth like a cornered feral creature and rage was now his prime emotion. It was a frightening transformation.

He began shaking his head and muttering to himself in a barely audible whisper;

'Treacherous little swine… after all I have done for him… he will have to pay.'

Realising these ravings probably referred to Gordon Hugill, Bob and Harry made a move towards the door, but Simpson then moved with lightning speed. He seized a knife from the drawer in front of him, which the police officers recognised as a butcher's steak knife. Before they were able to react, he leapt from his chair, barged past them and raced up the short flight of stairs. Frame and Maguire had been taken aback by the alacrity of Simpson's movements, but they quickly regained their verve and sprinted up the stairs behind them shouting to Hugill and Betty to 'run for it.'.

Whether Simpson's initial intention was simply to make his escape will probably never be known. Suffice to say, when he reached the top of the stairs and raced across the showroom, he saw the startled and terrified figures of Gordon Hugill and Betty Forster cowering on the sofa. They were mortified by the sudden appearance of the apparently demented figure of Simpson, clutching a butcher's steak knife; a potentially deadly weapon.

He stopped in his stride momentarily, then went berserk. He leapt across the room like a man possessed and grabbed hold of a bewildered Gordon Hugill by the front of his jacket and wrenched him to his feet. Simpson was salivating like a rabid dog and was clearly out of control. Howling like a banshee into Hugill's face, he screamed;

'You ungrateful, treacherous bastard. How dare you betray me? Have you any idea what you have done. Have you? Have you?'

Then, his strident voice rising in a fearful crescendo, to the horror and astonishment of Maguire and Frame and the mortal terror of Betty Forster, he took his knife and, slowly, deliberately and callously, he slit Gordon Hugill's throat. Hugill's attempted scream turned into a pitiful gurgle as his life's blood spurted across the room. The impact of the attack was immediate and fatal. Gordon Hugill slumped to the threadbare carpet, where he emitted a final agonised groan and died.

Betty Forster almost passed out as she uttered an impassioned and elongated scream before collapsing on the sofa in hysterics. Simpson, though, had not finished yet. As Maguire and Frame struggled to come to terms with the unexpected and fatal mayhem and the merciless slaying of Gordon Hugill, he grabbed the quivering and trembling figure of Betty Forster and held her in front of him as he placed the butcher's knife to her throat.

Using Betty as a human shield, Simpson made his way towards the door, seemingly intent on escaping from the carnage he had created. The wild look in his eyes as he attempted to accomplish his getaway did not bode well for his hostage. He had killed Gordon Hugill, he had most likely murdered Mary Bartlett and if the situation demanded it, he would not hesitate from disposing of Betty Forster as well. The poor girl was on the point of collapse. Fear and adrenalin were all that prevented her from passing out.

Simpson was barely in control of himself and his vociferous threats to kill his prisoner if he was not allowed to leave the scene were all-too-real. Harry forced himself to erase the image of the bleeding corpse of Gordon Hugill from his consciousness and managed a quiet and soothing tone as he attempted to mollify Simpson;

'Israel, this is not the way. You cannot…'

As his quarry looked at him contemptuously and brandished the knife. Harry broke off his sentence and with Simpson momentarily distracted, he launched himself, feet first, at Simpson's shins. It was a tackle which embodied all his competitive footballing instincts as he lashed his right foot with all the venom he could muster into the left shin of his opponent. It was not by any stretch of the imagination a tackle which would have escaped the wrath of a referee on the field of play, but needs must when the devil drives and in the circumstances, it was a fine piece of improvisation.

Simpson squealed in agony like a pig on a stick when he felt the impact of Harry's bludgeoning tackle and as he stumbled in reaction to the pain, Bob Frame brought another piece of sporting analogy to bear and walloped the hapless individual with a left hook of such power and timing that it would have done credit to the great Max Baer himself, who had defeated the Italian giant Primo Carnera to win the Heavyweight Championship of the World at Madison Square Garden in June. The referee had stopped the contest to protect Carnera from further punishment. There was no such compassion for Israel Simpson.

Harry Maguire grabbed the knife from the crumpled and semi-conscious heap on the floor. Bob Frame did his inadequate best to console and comfort the distraught Betty Forster, before taking the phone from the wall and calling the station for reinforcements as well as instructing the Duty Sergeant to contact Betty Forster's parents. They needed to know about the unbearable ordeal which had been inflicted on their daughter and come and take her home as soon as possible.

Nothing could be done for the unfortunate Gordon Hugill whose dead body was still oozing blood on the floor. The police surgeon would be contacted, and the body removed as soon as it was practicable. His parents would also have to be contacted and informed of their son's tragic demise. Harry and Bob had managed to recover a small measure of their equilibrium, though the full stress and upset associated with events like these would take a while to diminish

Simpson was clutching his damaged shin and mouthing obscenities and imprecations in the direction of his assailants. There would be a large measure of regret in the minds of both Maguire and Frame as they reflected on their inability to anticipate and avoid the gruesome slaying of Gordon Hugill, but they could take some solace from the fact that their joint efforts had certainly saved the life of Betty Forster. Harry handcuffed Simpson and stood over him as he alternated between cursing the two police officers and whimpering in pain.

A police van containing reinforcements arrived at the

scene in due course and Simpson was hauled away to be charged with the murder of Gordon Hugill as well as his part in the jewellery scam. The redoubtable PC Lloyd was deployed to stand watch over the scene of the crime and discourage the questions of inquisitive members of the general public. First, though, he was instructed to escort poor Betty Forster the few yards to Conlon's Florists where the owner would, doubtless, distribute tea and sympathy in large measures until the arrival of her parents.

Harry Maguire and Bob Frame were very subdued, thoughtful and quiet men when the police van deposited them back at the police station. The Desk Sergeant offered them his congratulations, which they barely acknowledged as they climbed the stairs leading to the Chief Superintendent's office. Walton was nobody's fool and he knew this was not the time for celebrations. He shook their hands with a peremptory 'well done lads' then indicated a couple of seats.

He poured two handsome measures of malt whisky from the cut glass decanter on his desk and passed them across without comment. The spirit was consumed with quiet gratitude and it soon worked its magic. The two officers were able to relax a little and between them they managed to produce a reasonable account of the events they had just experienced. Walton congratulated them again;

'Great job. Great job. Mickler and Goldberg were remanded in custody for a week by the magistrates this morning. Simpson is being charged and processed. He will be done for the Hugill murder as well as the attempted murder of Miss Forster, and for his part in the jewellery substitution business.'

The Chief Superintendent was a very satisfied man. These outcomes would do his reputation the power of good and for that he was grateful. However, he would not be 100% satisfied until he could also boast a result in the Mary Bartlett murder enquiry.

'Have you got enough to charge him with the Bartlett killing, do you think?'

Harry was not best pleased at the insensitivity of the question. He and Bob both knew what its motivation was, and they had little respect for the political side of the job at which their boss was so adept. He was still feeling the effects of the afternoon's events and he was grateful when Bob replied to the question;

'That was rather overtaken by events, sir, but if we are able to talk to him in the morning, I hope we will be able to tie things up. We have seen how irrationally he acts when he is provoked, and I doubt he will be at his chirpy and arrogant best by the time he has a night in the cells and he realises he is going to hang for the Hugill murder. We have the knife which killed Hugill and it is almost certainly the knife which also killed Mary Bartlett. I think he will accept that he has nothing to lose and will cough for the girl.'

'Good, good. We will talk about events again in the morning after you have interviewed Simpson.'

Harry visualised Walton rubbing his hands together with concealed glee under the table. The Spectre drew the short session to a merciful conclusion;

'Take yourselves off home now to your loved ones. Do your best to relax and have a good night's sleep'

That is easier said than achieved was the unspoken response which came to Harry's mind. A good sleep would certainly help but the mental scars would take time to heal. He and Bob would need to get themselves into the right frame of mind to finish the job tomorrow. Maybe then they could think about celebrating and begin the task of putting this afternoon's traumas into perspective.

CHAPTER SEVENTEEN

WEDNESDAY, 17TH OCTOBER

ON THE morning after Israel Simpson was arrested and charged with the murder of Gordon Hugill, he was brought from his cell in the basement of Market Street Police Station for formal questioning in the Interview Room on the first floor.

Essentially, he had no defence for the murder of Hugill and the attempted murder of Betty Forster since both Detective Constable Bob Frame and Detective Sergeant Harry Maguire had been present and witnessed the awful events of the afternoon. Indeed, it was Maguire's timely flying tackle and Frame's sweetly timed left hook which had prevented him from claiming the life of Betty Forster.

The object of this morning's interview was to discover more about the prisoner's alleged involvement in the original murder of Mary Bartlett. Recent developments had seen him replace Davy Conlon as the police's prime suspect. Frame and Maguire were cautiously optimistic of success and suspected that the only card Simpson could play with conviction was to reveal the part which jewellers Mickler and Goldberg had played in the massive jewellery scam with Simpson which had brought all three men substantial illegal rewards.

Normally a strikingly neat and dapper man, a night in the cells reflecting on his predicament had done little for Simpson's appearance. Limping from the aftereffects of Harry Maguire's lunging football tackle on his shin, he cut a less than elegant figure as he assumed his seat across the table from Maguire and Frame. He did, though, appear still to retain the vestiges of the dignity and self-confidence which had hitherto been his natural characteristics.

DC Frame began the interrogation;

'You realise, Mr. Simpson, that you are still under caution, having been charged with murder and attempted murder, and you are now the subject of further questions principally relating to another matter?'

It was a theoretical question to which Simpson offered a nod of the head by way of assent.

'You are, of course, entitled to have a lawyer present and we will adjourn this session while the necessary arrangements are made if you so desire.'

'That will not be necessary, Detective Constable. I am content to answer your questions to the best of my ability.'

In other circumstances this reply would have been regarded as extraordinarily foolhardy, but during the course of their dealings with this particular individual the investigating officers had realised beyond doubt that Israel Simpson was no ordinary person.

It would be interesting to discover whether the marked change in his appearance overnight was matched by a change in his demeanour. His hair, which until now had been fastidiously groomed, appeared unkempt and unwashed. His perennial white shirt had become grubby, sweaty and bedraggled. His normally immaculately pressed black trousers had the appearance of those of a vagrant who had spent the night sleeping on a park bench and his formerly highly polished and shiny shoes appeared scuffed and worn. In short, he had descended overnight into a downtrodden replica of his former self.

Yet, there was still the semblance of a presence about him. His air of confidence and poise had certainly diminished, but he still appeared to have the capability of taking care of himself intellectually even in his perilous plight. Not for him the hunched and cowed figure of a man with no future. He sat upright, facing his accusers. There was no naked defiance, but he exuded an inner belief which belied his situation.

'You will appreciate,' Bob continued, 'that aside from the matters with which you have already been charged, we are still investigating the outstanding matter of the death of Mary Bartlett, the flower girl. The knife you were carrying yesterday and with which you killed Gordon Hugill, is a match for the butcher's steak knife which was used to murder young Mary. Do you have any observation to make on that?'

Simpson's reply was almost perky, as if he was thinking that if this was all they had, he need not worry unduly;

'Only, Constable, that such knives are commonplace, especially in an environment like the Grainger Market where butchery is the predominant means of employment. There are probably twenty or thirty butchers in there who carry a steak knife as a tool of their trade.'

'That is as maybe,' Bob replied, unruffled by the prisoner's calm response, 'but such knives are not routinely carried by jewellers of who there are less than a handful in the market of which you are one.'

A brief flicker of self-doubt passed across Simpson's face. This was far from being one of DC Frame's out-of-the-blue stunning observations, capable of turning a case on its head. It was a routine comment, but Simpson's minimal change of expression had illustrated the fragile nature of his defence. Bob followed up his perceived advantage quickly;

'It is still a fact that your knife killed Gordon Hugill and there is more than a possibility it was also used on Mary Bartlett. Let me turn now to your opportunity, movements and motivation on the night of that young lady's death. We have been able to establish that Mary tripped and knocked herself out on the market floor. She landed face down on the metal grill above the basement of your premises. By your own admission, you were working in your basement that night, most likely on another of the stones which you have been fashioning as part of your scheme with Mickler and Goldberg. It was not quite dark in the market where the lights were still burning and if you glanced up you could not help but see her. That gave you the opportunity, and it is my conviction that you mistakenly thought the woman was watching you, spying on you through the grill as you worked on the ring. When you take into account the huge amount of money involved in your racket, you could not afford to have anyone knowing what you were up to. The scam was simply too highly rewarded and in the heat of the moment you decided the person you thought was spying on you had to be disposed of.

'You grabbed an old sheet or blanket from your workshop, took your knife from the drawer and rushed upstairs. While the poor woman was recovering consciousness, you wrapped the sheet around her and stabbed her in the back with the butcher's knife. It was then you realised, no doubt to your horror, the error of your ways. You recognised your victim as the girl from Conlon's shop. You fished in her pocket and found the shop keys, which was a stroke of luck, then you carried her body the few yards to the florists. You opened the door and carried her corpse inside. You sat her on a chair and removed the sheet. You then closed the shop door and then you returned, with the sheet, to your workshop. You collected your overcoat and your freemason's case and slipped quickly and unobtrusively out of the market. You then made your way to the taxi stand where you met your friend Davy Conlon. The pair of you set off for your lodge meeting.

'Poor Mary Bartlett was not a spy or a snooper. She was simply an ordinary, decent young woman who happened to trip and fall face down in such a way as to make you think she was an inquisitive and troublesome person who was placing your despicably dishonest money-making racket in jeopardy. She was in a position caused by mishap not mischief and she paid the highest price when you took her life. It is almost unimaginable that a man could be so evil. You let your avarice and greed lead you to panic and you took an innocent life without compunction.'

Bob Frame had presented Simpson with a compelling indictment of his behaviour but, while Simpson looked shaken, he was not broken. It was time for Bob to deliver the show-stopping finale he had produced to excellent effect on previous occasions. He sent his golden arrow straight to Simpson's heart, in a stroke, insinuating that the police were aware of his murky and violent past;

'I am afraid the game is up, it is time to come clean, Reuben.'

Such was the accuracy and inevitability of Bob Frame's summary of the killing of Mary Bartlett that Simpson had remained silent throughout. He disputed nothing. He simply allowed himself a small and sad smile of resignation. The coup-de-grace that was the revealing of his proper name, seemed finally to convince him that protest was futile. He did not physically hold his hands up, but he might as well have done. When Bob looked up from his notes and met Simpson's eyes, he knew the chase was over;

'Well,' he said in a tone which implied this was the end game, 'what do you have to say for yourself?'

'You seem to have got it just about right, Detective Constable,' said Simpson resignedly. 'I congratulate you. I thought I saw the young woman staring down at me. It was dusk and I did not recognise her. As you rightly say, I thought I was being spied on and I admit I panicked. If I had stopped to think I would have had nothing to worry about, but with so much money involved I think I subconsciously thought it was a chance worth taking.

'When I realised what I had done, I was mortified but there was nothing I could do except behave normally. That was why I came straight to you with my statement. Incidentally, you were also correct in assuming I was working on another ring, which was probably a factor in my decision. I can only say I am sorry for the girl's family and it goes without saying I deeply regret my actions.'

'So, you admit you were responsible for the murder of Mary Bartlett as well as the killing of Gordon Hugill and the attempted murder of Betty Forster?'

'I am afraid I do.'

'Well, you will of course be formally charged with the murder of Mary Bartlett. However, there are other matters we still need to talk about. Would you like to take a break at this point?'

'Do you know, Detective Constable Frame, I think I would. Would it be possible to have a cup of tea?'

Simpson's remorse at his senseless killing of Mary Bartlett seemed genuine but his casual request for a cup of tea at that juncture was another strange twist, and a further indication of the deep and diverse nature of the man.

The tea was delivered, and Bob Frame had enjoyed a quick cigarette before he resumed his interrogation.

'Thank you for the refreshment, Mr. Frame. With your permission I would like to sign a statement now and accept the consequences of my actions. I can have no complaints, though I do regret the way things have turned out.'

Once again, Simpson had revealed his unpredictability. He would certainly go to the gallows for the murders of Mary Bartlett and Gordon Hugill and, rather than protest his innocence in the face of overwhelming evidence, he appeared to be raising the white flag of defeat. It did not seem to fit with a man of his intellect, quick thinking and deviousness. Bob was happy to comply with his request, however, secure in the knowledge that the final curtain was close.

'Very well. I am happy for you to lead the conversation for now. Would you prefer me to call you Reuben or Israel?'

'I have no preference. I think we are beyond the niceties now, Detective Constable. Let me first just say one thing about my part in the jewellery caper. I think it would be accurate to say that Mickler, Goldman and myself were equal partners in the enterprise. Quite simply, I approached them with the idea, and they took it on board willingly. We profited to the tune of anything between £200 and £500 on each transaction and over the years I suppose we must have pulled the same stunt perhaps 25 times. That is a great deal of money. I would estimate that we cleared at least £10,000 which was divided more or less equally between us. They actually took a bigger cut after they became aware of my previous life, as it were, and began blackmailing me.

'I have a savings account containing £2,500, so you can work it out. That is the equivalent of an artisan's wages for ten years! I tell you this not out of vindictiveness but out of fairness. They may attempt to lay the blame at my door, but justice has to be done. They will have bank accounts in excess of mine and that will provide the proof.

'As far as the other matters are concerned, it would be both fatuous and pointless of me to do other than admit the killing of Gorgon Hugill and the attempted murder of Betty Forster. I could have offered a rather more staunch defence of the charge regarding Mary Bartlett, but what would be the point? We know I was responsible for that as well.

'Finally, I wish to apologise most profusely for the pain

I have caused to the loved ones of my victims. I do not ask for their forgiveness for what I have done is unforgiveable. I will say no more, Detective Constable. For there is no more to be said.'

With that Israel Simpson, alias Reuben Silverman, folded his arms, closed his eyes briefly and awaited his fate.

It had all ended with rather more of a whimper than a storm. The high drama had been acted out in Israel Simpson's' workshop the previous day. Nevertheless. His confession to the murder of Mary Bartlett had brought matters to a very satisfactory conclusion after the dramas of the last couple of weeks. There were some loose ends to tie up. The expectation was that Simpson/Silverman would plead guilty to all charges. Mickler and Goldberg would go on trial for fraud and doubtless be sent to prison for several years. In the short term, Davy Conlon would be informed that he was no longer regarded as a suspect in the Mary Bartlett case.

Harry Maguire and Bob Frame would, as a matter of priority and in keeping with the promise they had made at Mary's funeral, visit Mrs. Bartlett and inform her that her daughter's killer had been arrested and charged. Hopefully, that would allow her to begin to find closure. Betty Forster would need the loving care of her parents to overcome the traumas she had endured and in time would need to seek alternative employment.

The young couple whose ring had been such a feature of the case would be consulting their insurers. They would expect to have the option of having the original ring restored to them. Whether it now carried too many negative connotations would be for them to decide. Maybe they would take the pragmatic course and keep the copy since it was such a convincing replica and spend the balance of the insurance money on something else!

All of which left Danny Veitch. Without his intervention and information there was every likelihood the Bartlett murder would not have been solved. Pauline Conlon would probably never agree, but in the eyes of Detective Sergeant Harry Maguire and Detective Constable Bob Frame Danny Veitch was a diamond…in a manner of speaking.

EPILOGUE

THURSDAY 18TH OCTOBER

THE MORNING following Israel Simpson's confession to the murders of Mary Bartlett and Gordon Hugill, which had brought to an end a harrowing and hazardous investigation, lacked the gloom and dampness which normally greeted Bob Frame as he lit his first cigarette of the day and waited for his friend and colleague Harry Maguire at the bottom of Bulmer Street. There was actually a hint of early morning brightness and the possibility of a sunny October day in prospect. That would certainly be in keeping with the mood of the Scotsman after the recent triumph enjoyed by himself and Harry Maguire.

Usually, it was Harry's loping footsteps on the cobble stones and the Detective Sergeant's cheerful whistling which broke the silence, but this morning Bob Frame himself was in a chirpy musical mood. Not for him, though, the tunes of the day favoured by Harry Maguire. It was a favourite song of his homeland, Robert Burns, 'My Love is Like a Red, Red Rose,' which emanated quietly and, it has to be conceded, with a more than pleasant mellifluence, from the proud Scot's lips as he waited for his mate. It was a brief and uncharacteristic interlude, quickly interrupted by Harry's arrival;

'Morning, Bob.'

'Morning, Guv.'

'Nice morning.'

'Very pleasant.'

No departure, then, from the usual brief and clipped early morning exchanges as they set off down Darn Crook towards the Market Street Police Station which was their workplace. They did, however, allow themselves rather more casual conversation than was their usual habit. There was a natural desire for both men to reflect on the happenings of the last few days, but they avoided triumphalism and instead speculated on what lay ahead.

'I expect the Spectre will want to see us.'

'Bound to.'

'We will need to grab a cuppa in the canteen before we go upstairs, then.'

'Agreed.'

Fortified by their morning brew, they made their way up the now familiar marble staircase of the recently opened police station where they had so spectacularly proved themselves as murder investigators.

Before they reached the haven of their office, the door of Chief Superintendent Ken Walton's office opened and then the tall, gaunt and immaculate figure of the man himself appeared. It was a daily ritual. On a good day they would sneak past without interruption but, more often than not, the boss anticipated their arrival and was waiting to greet them.

'Good morning, gentlemen,' was at least a more amiable

greeting than the usual. 'You two, in here now.' The mood about the place was bound to be upbeat in the circumstances and for the first time either man could recall, there was actually something resembling a smile on Walton's drawn and pale face. Affability was not his strongest suit, and this was as clear an indication as they would get that a good day lay ahead.

'Good morning, sir.'

'A word, if you would.'

'Yes, sir.'

They stepped into their boss's palatial office and were invited to sit down; another indication of the positive light which was shining on the two detectives. There was no doubt at all that they had boosted their own reputations and their colleagues were basking in the reflected glory.

'I expect you two are feeling mighty pleased with yourselves this morning?'

'Well, sir...'

'Never mind that. I told you at the outset of this investigation that I was placing the pair of you in charge as much because I had no choice due to staffing shortages as for any other reason. However, I also said, as I am sure you will recall, that I had faith in your ability to solve the case. You have more than justified my faith in you both, so first things first. Congratulations on a job extremely well done.

'I also predicted that a successful outcome would reflect well on the station and it would bring credit all round, which it has. I have already received a call this morning from the Chief Constable, congratulating the squad and passing on his particular thanks to you two for the professional way in which you have handled the case. The Chief Constable and I have also had a conversation about what best to do with you now. As you know, we are still short of bodies in the squad.

'We are on the brink of appointing a new Detective Superintendent which will be a big help in terms of senior administration, but there is still no sign of the Detective Chief Inspector returning. So, this is what has been decided. As a reward for your excellent work on the Bartlett case, Maguire, you are being recommended for the post of Acting Detective Inspector and you, Frame, will be elevated to the rank of Acting Detective Sergeant.'

'Thank you, sir!' came the simultaneous responses of the delighted pair. Walton cut them short;

'Do not get carried away with yourselves. I must emphasise the word 'acting' in both cases. That means what it says, and the arrangement will be reviewed in three months, at which time a decision will be taken whether to extend your roles, make them permanent, or have you return to your present ranks. Understood?'

'Yes, sir.'

The Chief Superintendent rose from his chair and walked across the plush Axminster carpet in their direction. They stood to meet him as he extended his hand.

'Congratulations, lads. I am proud of you. This is a deserved opportunity and I don't expect you to let me down. Incidentally, it has also been decided that in light of his excellent support work, and based on a glowing report from yourselves, PC Lloyd will be transferred to the detective division, so you will have an extra pair of hands at your disposal. Now, get yourselves downstairs to the canteen and treat yourselves to a proper breakfast at my expense. Report back here in an hour so I can talk you through your revised duties.'

'Yes, sir, thank you sir,' they stammered as they narrowly avoided tripping over each other on the way out.

Neither Harry Maguire or Bob Frame was a particularly demonstrative person, but they allowed themselves a spontaneous slap on the back as Chief Superintendent Walton closed his door behind them. This was a great boost to both of their careers, even if it did only last for three months, which they would be doing their level best to prevent. Not only did the promotion carry with it a very welcome rise in pay, which would go down extremely well with Mrs. Maguire and Mrs. Frame, but their standing in the force would be greatly enhanced.

Following Mr. Walton's instruction, they selected a handsome breakfast apiece which they consumed at their leisure while accepting the congratulations of sundry of their colleagues on their success in the Bartlett case. They enjoyed a leisurely cigarette before returning, replete, to the Chief's office. As they approached, the beaming figure of PC Lloyd stepped out. Another slap on the back and appropriate congratulations followed before they knocked on Walton's door to receive their new briefing.

In reality, their new responsibilities were not fundamentally different, except they were now officially the force's front-line investigating officers in the event of any serious crime, including murder. The meeting was short and the Chief Superintendent brought it to a conclusion by congratulating them yet again before showing them out of his office.

Closing the door in their wake, he sat back in his chair and selected a handsome cigar from the humidor on his desk. Then, he congratulated himself, not for the first time in the last 24 hours, on his own good fortune. He had been the recipient of considerable kudos from those in high places and was likely to continue doing so. His gamble on the two rookies had paid off handsomely.

Acting Detective Inspector Harry Maguire and Acting Detective Sergeant Bob Frame sat at their desks in their office attempting unsuccessfully to restrain the grins on their faces. They were euphoric at the morning's news as they waited for the first action of the day to come their way. They did not have to wait long. Detective Constable Lloyd, also sitting on cloud nine as a result of his transfer to the detective unit, put down the phone after taking their first call of the morning and called across;

'Excuse me, Guv, there is a message here about someone having been beaten up. Apparently, the body of a middle-aged man has been discovered in the St. Andrew's churchyard on Newgate Street. He appears to be in a bad way.'

'Do we have any details? Identity or anything?' Harry asked.

'Not yet, Guv, just that he is in a bit of a state. Apparently, a member of the public informed a beat bobby and he has organised an ambulance to take the victim to the Infirmary.'

'Very well, Constable, Harry said, 'we have nothing else scheduled for the morning so we may as well take ourselves across and see what it is all about. It will be a nice, routine start to our first day. Besides, Mary Bartlett's mother lives just across the road. We can call and let her know the good news about Israel Simpson at the same time'

It took about twenty minutes to walk from the police station to the Royal Victoria Infirmary on Queen Victoria Road. They informed Ken Walton of their intentions and left Lloyd in charge of matters. Then they set off at a brisk and purposeful pace. It was nearly ten o'clock in the morning and the sun had kept its promise to shine, so it was a slightly perspiring pair of policemen who arrived at the main entrance of the hospital. They presented themselves at the reception area and asked the duty clerk for details of the recently admitted patient who had been the victim of an assault in the town centre.

'Yes, gentlemen, he was brought in about a half an hour ago. The doctor will probably be seeing to him now. If you make your way down the corridor and take the first turning on your right, that will take you to the out-patients' department. Mr. Conlon should be in there.'

Conlon? Surely not. Bob and Harry were rocked on their heels. Could their victim possibly be Davy Conlon, the sleazy bookmaker who had featured so prominently in their recent case? There was only one way to find out and they almost ran the short distance to out-patients. They were greeted by a pretty, fair-haired young nurse who they just about avoided bumping into in their haste.

'Can I help you, gentlemen,' she asked politely, with a smile on her more than pleasant face.

Harry and Bob produced their warrant cards and said they were looking into the assault on someone earlier that morning in St. Andrew's churchyard who had recently been admitted.

'Mr. Conlon? If you care to take a seat, I will let the doctor know you are here.'

'What do you make of this lot, Bob?'

'I would hazard an educated guess that if it is our man Davy, there might be a lady and an outraged husband involved!'

A white-coated doctor introduced himself and explained that the patient had suffered a severe beating. He would need treatment and would be required to remain in hospital under observation for at least 24 hours. However, he was conscious, and they could speak to him provided they kept it brief.

Davy Conlon was propped up by pillows on an emergency bed behind a privacy curtain. It was obvious he had been badly beaten and bruising was beginning to appear on his already swollen face. His lip was split, and he had the makings of a very impressive black eye.

'Well, Davy,' Bob Frame smirked, 'you are a proper sight for sore eyes. Someone catch up with you at last, did they? They certainly seem to have given you a good going-over.'

Davy winced in obvious pain as he leaned forward to reply;

'You can bloody well say that again. They think I have broken two ribs. I am in agony and they've given me nowt for it.'

Bob was enjoying this;

'That is a disgrace, Davy, you should complain,' he said sarcastically, 'Still, that should teach you not to be such a naughty boy.

Despite his pain and discomfort, Conlon still managed to be outraged;

'The bloody woman told me her husband was away in the Merchant Navy for two weeks so the coast would be clear,' he said indignantly, 'lying cow.'

Harry and Bob were close to hysterics. They had no sympathy at all for Conlon's predicament and were actually pleased he had received his just desserts at last.

Bob returned to the fray;

'Would I be right in thinking you don't wish to press charges?' he almost spluttered

'Not bloody likely!'

Bob was about to rub more salt into Conlon's not insignificant wounds:

'You do realise we will have to inform your missus, don't you?'

The wretched man groaned agonisingly at the prospect and the officers, having had their share of fun at his expense, decided enough was enough. They made a quick note of the nature of his injuries and his desire not to take the matter any further. Davy could be left to stew in his own juice. Bob thanked the nurse for her help, and they set off to see Mrs. Bartlett.

As they stepped out from the imposing portico of the hospital, Bob and Harry were within two minutes of Terrace Place. It was a neat row of terraced houses which led from Leazes Park Road to the imposing edifice which was known to the fans as the 'popular side', of St. James' Park. They had this one piece of unfinished business to attend to before they went to the Grainger Market to inform Pauline Conlon of her philandering husband's most recent unfortunate mishap.

Dorothy Bartlett occupied the third house on the right as they turned into Terrace Place. Their errand was a strange one. They were here to inform the lady that the monster who had killed her daughter had been arrested and charged, but neither man felt entirely comfortable with the situation.

They had only met Mrs. Bartlett once, at her daughter's funeral, and they were conscious of the fact that she was a lady still deep in mourning for the loss of her only child. They would have felt very much more relaxed if they had a female police officer with them to offer feminine solace to the grieving mother. The fact was, though, that the police force was almost exclusively a male reserve. Campaigns to recruit female officers were gathering momentum, as well as popular support, but, as yet, the necessary legislation was not on the statute book.

Harry knocked on the door and after a short delay, footsteps could be heard, and a timorous voice enquired;

'Who is it?'

'It's the police, Mrs Bartlett. We have some news for you.'

The pulling back of a bolt and the lifting of a latch were followed by the slow opening of the door. Dorothy Bartlett had discarded her mourning black and wore a housewife's work apron over a dark blue dress. She was a short, neat woman with greying hair who held herself erect as she looked them over a little apprehensively.

'Hello, Mrs. Bartlett,' Harry began, 'we are sorry to disturb you, but there has been a substantial development in the search for Mary's killer. You probably remember us from

Mary's funeral. I am Detective Sergeant Maguire, and this is my colleague DC Frame. We promised that when we had some positive news we would get in touch with you straight away. Do you mind if we come in for a few minutes?'

Dorothy was uncertain how to react and fell back on the natural courtesy and respect for authority which most people in her station in life displayed;

'Come in, come in. I will put the kettle on and make a pot of tea.'

She showed Harry and Bob to a sofa with a pretty floral cover and went to busy herself in the kitchen, returning a few minutes later bearing a tray on which there was a teapot, a couple of cups and saucers, a small white milk jug with a gold rim and a matching sugar bowl. She then returned to the kitchen and fetched a cup for herself and a plate on which were half a dozen custard cream biscuits.

The preparing of the refreshments seemed to have calmed her. She was on familiar ground in her own home as she poured the tea and composed herself on a chair opposite her two visitors and folded her arms;

'Help yourselves to milk and sugar and a biscuit, gentlemen,' she invited them, then waited for their next move.

The room was neat, spotlessly clean, and cosy and there was a pleasant odour of lavender. It was a cared-for house and Dorothy Bartlett was showing commendable composure.

'Let me give you the good news, Mrs Bartlett,' Bob Frame began, 'if there can be good news in the circumstances. We have arrested and charged someone with Mary's murder, and he has confessed. We wanted you to know straight away.'

Mrs. Bartlett gulped, fumbled in her apron pocket for a handkerchief and dabbed at the tears which were forming in her eyes;

'Who did it? Who killed my Mary, Mr. Frame?'

'It was a man called Israel Simpson, Mrs, Bartlett, 'he had a small jewellery shop not far from where Mary's body was found.'

Mrs. Bartlett said nothing. She stood up and removed a small necklace from around her neck. She walked to the fire and threw the necklace into the flames then she gathered herself for a few moments and returned to her chair.

'I'm so sorry, gentlemen. I bought that necklace at Simpson's the Jeweller's. It was second hand and it didn't cost much, but I was taken by it at the time. I couldn't bear to wear it again after what you have told me.'

She gathered herself and asked how they had found out who had committed the crime. Bob thought it best not to tell Mrs. Bartlett the full circumstances of Simpson's arrest and the murder of Gordon Hugill. She would find that out soon enough and he contented himself with a bland and brief outline of the forensic evidence which seemed to satisfy her.

'But why? I don't understand. Mary wouldn't hurt a fly. Why would he do this horrible thing?

'I'm sorry to say Mary was the victim of circumstances, Mrs. Bartlett. She was in the wrong place at the wrong time.'

Dorothy took a deep breath and closed her eyes before exhaling slowly;

'It's such a waste,' she whispered. 'but I'm relieved it's over.

This has been an awful ordeal for me, gentlemen, as you can imagine. I knew I would never find rest until Mary's killer was brought to justice. Thank you so much. What will happen to him now?'

'Well,' said Bob, 'he has confessed, so he will plead guilty at his trial and he will be hanged.'

'I'm a churchgoer, gentlemen,' said Dorothy, 'and Christians are taught forgiveness but I won't ever be able to find it in my heart to show any compassion to that monster for taking my Mary from me.'

She spoke with dignity and feeling. It was clear that while this was a lady of small stature, Dorothy Bartlett was a strong woman;

'I am still trying to take it in. I know I will never get over it, of course. I lost my husband at the end of the war, you know.'

She pointed at a sepia photograph of a young man wearing an able seaman's uniform which stood on the mantlepiece;

'My Norman was taken from me when his ship went down in 1918. I have learned to accept it, but I still miss him and losing Mary as well is so hard to take.'

The poor lady was struggling to hold herself together and Bob reached across and placed his hand over hers;

'You are very brave, Mrs. Bartlett, and I hope you will be able to come to terms with your dreadful loss in due course now you know the name of the person who took Mary from you and that he will receive the punishment he deserves. If there is anything we can do, please ask.'

'You have done what you needed to do, son, by catching this evil creature. It will take a while for me to get myself together, I know that, but I have my sister and brother-in-law to rely on. They have been marvellous. Then there is my job. I work over at the school, you know, and Miss Cooper has been so kind. It's half term this week and I will be going back next Monday. Life goes on. I have cried my tears for my little girl, though I expect I will cry some more. I will have to find a way to be strong.'

Harry felt a lump in his throat. For Dorothy Bartlett to lose both of her loved ones in tragic circumstances was an unimaginably cruel twist of fate. His heart went out to her. He told her she would be informed when Simpson went on trial. She would be under no obligation to attend. They lingered a while over their tea and biscuits before thanking her for her hospitality, then they said their goodbyes, giving her an awkward hug.

'Bye, bye, lads. Thank you so much for coming and God bless you for all you have done.'

It was a poignant parting. Bob and Harry were both emotional as they set off on their way to the Grainger Market to see Pauline Conlon.

'She is holding up remarkably well and she seems to have good people around her, but she has a long, hard road to travel,' Bob observed. 'When Simpson goes to the gallows, she may find peace in her heart, poor soul.'

The looming prospect of heaping greater ignominy on Davy Conlon by informing his wife of his recent misfortune went some way to lifting the spirits of the two detectives, and they picked up their pace and added a small measure of jauntiness to their steps as the Grainger Market came into view.

Pauline was her ebullient self;

'I thought the case was closed. All done and dusted, and that swine locked away,' she announced bitterly when they presented themselves at the doorway of her shop.

'So it is, Mrs. Conlon,' Harry confirmed. 'I am afraid we are here on another matter. We have just been to the RVI to investigate a nasty assault case. I'm sorry to have to inform you the victim was your Davy.'

Pauline Conlon was taken aback by the news, but there was certainly no hint of compassion in her response;

'What? What has the stupid bugger been up to now, for goodness sake?'

'I am sorry to tell you he has some nasty facial injuries and the probability of broken ribs. They are keeping him in.'

'Who did it? Somebody's husband I suppose.'

'We don't know,' Harry lied. Davy was in enough trouble. 'He is keeping very quiet on that subject. We are just here to let you know what has happened. He is in the Accident and Emergency wing and we can arrange for you to be taken to the hospital to see him, if you like.'

'Don't be ridiculous, Mr. Maguire. Live by the sword, perish by the sword, I say. Let him get on with it. It's his own stupid fault. I have a business to run. As long as he's not critically injured, I'll go and see him during evening visiting hours. Not that he can expect any sympathy. Thank you for letting me know. Can the two of you just wait there a moment?'

Without waiting for a reply, she breezed into the back room of the shop, returning almost instantly holding an impressive bunch of flowers in each hand;

'I know you lads are not supposed to accept gifts from members of the public, Mr. Maguire, but the two of you were so kind to me over poor Mary and now taking the trouble to come and tell me about Davy. These are not for you, they are for your wives, and thank you so much for your trouble.'

She hustled the pair of them out of the shop, flowers and all, without giving them time to protest. Pauline Conlon, despite her domineering nature, had a heart, perhaps not of gold, but maybe of silver. Her husband, though, might have cause to think it was made of stone a few hours from now.

Harry and Bob made their way sheepishly through the Grainger Market and back to the police station, trying their best the pretend that the flowers they were carrying did not exist. The reactions of their colleagues when they walked into the station can be imagined.

'Lovely flowers, ladies. What did you do to get those?' That was by a distance the least ribald of the comments they received as they sprinted upstairs to their office.

'I think I could get used to this acting-up lark, Guv,' Bob Frame joked as they sat down and got their breath back, 'A pay rise and a bunch of flowers to take home to Ena on the first day. It's great.'

'Make the most of it, Bob,' was Harry's more pragmatic reply, 'It will not always be like this.'

Right on cue he was proved correct. The door opened without ceremony and the imposing figure of Chief Superintendent Walton appeared;

'My office, you two, now,' came his peremptory command.

There was no friendly handshake this time, just a very

solid reminder that it was now business as usual. No sooner had they closed the boss's door than he launched into his more familiar persona;

'Never mind that clown Conlon and bunches of flowers. This is not the Royal Variety Show. Speaking of which, I need the pair of you to get yourselves along to Percy Street at the double. Some garbled story about a crime having been committed at the Palace Theatre, and it being serious. It seems they are rehearsing for the pantomime already, so God knows what it's all about. Possibly Aladdin has rubbed his wonderful lamp too hard and vanished, or maybe somebody has shot the rear end of the cow up the arse. Get yourselves up there and sort it out...Ho! Ho! Ho!'

Two weeks later, the local evening paper screamed the headline;

CHILD SLAYER SUICIDE SENSATION

The front page story read;

'47 year old Israel Simpson who was awaiting trial for the murders of florist Mary Bartlett and jeweller's apprentice Gordon Hugill in Newcastle's Grainger Market to which he had confessed to police, has been found dead, hanging in his prison cell. He was also involved in an alleged jewellery scam worth hundreds of pounds for which his former employers, Joshua Mickler and Samuel Goldberg, are also awaiting trial. Acting Detective Inspector Harry Maguire, the chief investigating officer on the case declined to comment.'

ACKNOWLEDGEMENTS

A word or two about names first.

Both generations of the Frame's and the Maguire's lived in Bulmer Street from the 1940's to the early 1960's. Bob Frame and Harry Maguire were my favourite uncles, along with Uncle Joe who lived in Birmingham. They were born in the early 1920's and would have been in their teens in 1934. Neither was a policeman. Harry was an electrician and Bob was a motor mechanic. I took them as models for my detectives out of lifelong affection and because they seemed to fit the characters I had created in terms of their temperaments, and dispositions.

Mary Bartlett, Raymond Hoult and Ken Walton were names which came to me from my formative years and seem to fit the characters. I have not had contact with any of them for over sixty years. If a copy of the book should fall into any of their laps. I hope they will forgive the liberty. None of them are villains of the piece. Mrs. Veitch was the caretaker of St Andrew's Church Hall. She was a redoubtable and conscientious person and she had a son called Danny. I knew them only slightly, but they were decent people. Miss Cooper, whose name I gave to the character who recommended Mary to Pauline, was my Headmistress in infant school. She was a spinster who lived in a posh house at the top of our street and I was terrified of her.

I could find no trace of there ever having been jewellery shops named Mickler and Goldberg or Simpson's, or a Conlon's Florist's in the history of the Grainger Market. The characters with these names are fictional and any resemblance to real people is purely coincidental. The tunnels in the basement of the Grainger Market still exist. They were constructed in the 1930's and their purpose remains the subject of speculation. They may be visited as part of official tours of the market by Newcastle City guides.

The bill of boxing fayre described was the actual bill on that specific night and the opening round knockout in the first contest did happen. It is also recorded that the regular meetings of jewellers at a specific table in Carrick's café took place. The newspaper shop on Gallowgate was known to me the 1950's when I was a boy and I remember some of the footballers of the day being there after training.

I am especially indebted to the following;

Mike Scott and Freda Thompson; Newcastle City Guides and Grainger Market experts, for background information.

Karl Wilson at VJW Jewellers in the Grainger Market for details of the locations of tunnels and shop basements.

Malcolm Smith for reminding me of the names of the Ordnance Arms and Varley's Fish and Chips.

Harry Bradley for his insights into the workings of the jewellery trade.

Bill Gibson for his steadfast support and encouragement and his limitless coterie of contacts.

There are two books written about the Grainger Market which proved to be useful points of reference;

'The Grainger Market; The People's History' by Yvonne Young.

'150 Years of the Grainger Market 1835-1985.' The Grainger Market Arcade Traders' Association. Newcastle City Libraries.

Grainger Street has always been a sophisticated part of town and the Grainger Market was a warm and welcoming place I have known well from childhood. I have passed through the market hundreds and hundreds of times. Both sets of grandparents lived in Bulmer Street. The local trolley bus from our house in Jesmond stopped just outside the market. Transported in a pram, then a push chair and in time as a hand-held toddler, before ultimately becoming old enough to make the journey unaccompanied, I continued those walks throughout my teens and beyond into early adulthood. Where before I had held my Mam's hand as I stood on tiptoe gazing at the toys, games and models in the toyshop, I graduated in time to browsing in the record shop and spending what little money I had on second-hand book bargains in Robinson's. Over the years I came to know some of the stall holders; butchers who had been at school with Mam, former class mates of my parents, apprentice butchers from my halcyon days at St Andrew's youth club. It was very familiar ground, which I trod to and from my grandparents houses in Bulmer Street.

It was a place full of character and characters, a familiar ground providing a fun experience, but despite its overall feeling of warmth and wellbeing there was a slight hint of the unknown which made it an exciting place with a small frisson, a tiny tinge of menace and danger. It had the potential to be a dangerous place though I personally always felt safe and secure there.

It was while I was recalling the events of The Kaleidoscope the following morning to my children Jonathan, Caroline and Christian I realised I had been guided to the location of the detective story I had always wanted to write from the early days of primary school compositions and grammar school essays and college dissertations. These I had written with reasonable success and satisfaction. In my teaching career I had taken massive pleasure from encouraging creative writing in my pupils.

I had written newspaper and magazine articles and a couple of works of non-fiction. I had not, however, achieved the target I had periodically set myself over the years of writing a crime novel. My problem was an inability to imagine an original plot and location and I had discarded the notion on more than one occasion after abortive beginnings.

Now, though, I had an overwhelming feeling that my kaleidoscopic experience had provided the solution. I would set my story in the Grainger Market in the 1930s and allow the plot to emerge. The result was The Grainger Market Murders.

My biggest debt of all goes to my lovely daughter Caroline. Apart from being at my side when I underwent the course of chemotherapy which ultimately saved my bacon, she expressed a wish to step down from her original role of co-author because of other commitments and instead became my editor. This role she undertook with diligence, intelligence and perception despite the competing demands of raising a family, completing her MA in Creative Writing and working three days a week at the University of Northumbria as well as pursuing her own writing ambitions. I am in awe of her various talents and her stamina and I love her dearly.